When Ray Grass died he left an estate worth millions, a valuable collection of firearms and a will full of his own mischievous sense of fun. He had been an enthusiastic sportsman and when the fatal accident enquiry brought in a verdict of accidental death, due to his carrying a loaded gun while climbing a fence, his neighbours and acquaintances shook their heads sadly at the folly of rich bachelors.

But for some of his friends such carelessness was uncharacteristic, so reluctantly (but with an eye on the gun collection) Keith Calder agreed to accompany the solicitor, Enterkin, to Grass's estate and make his own enquiries.

Once Calder learnt the detailed facts of the 'accidental' death, he knew the verdict had been wrong and set about trying to prove the truth. Not an easy task, since he was surrounded by a large number of people who, in very individual and bizarre ways, would benefit hugely from Grass's death.

He discovered that one of the policemen on the case shared his doubts. As they piece together the events of the death they find more than one murder and run into grave danger.

Gerald Hammond has established a popular reputation with the adventures of Keith Calder, and this new one contains all the best ingredients – gunlore, gamesmanship, poaching, womanising, a sharp sense of humour and sudden death.

FAIR GAME

Gerald Hammond

Macmillan

ISBN 0 333 32768 3

First published 1982 by
MACMILLAN LONDON LIMITED
London and Basingstoke
Associated companies in Auckland, Dallas, Delhi,
Dublin, Hong Kong, Johannesburg, Lagos, Manzini, Melbourne,
Nairobi, New York, Singapore, Tokyo,
Washington and Zaria

Typeset in Great Britain by
MB GRAPHIC SERVICES LIMITED
Bovingdon, Hertfordshire

Printed in Great Britain by
THE ANCHOR PRESS LIMITED
Tiptree, Essex

Bound in Great Britain by
WM. BRENDON AND SON LIMITED
Tiptree, Essex

Every character in this book is intended to be wholly fictitious.

In one other way I have departed from strict verisimilitude: any writer who places his tales in an area where dialect is spoken confronts himself with a number of choices. He may write as if his characters all spoke English as uttered by Her Majesty or by the BBC. At the other extreme, and to the great tedium of his readers, he may attempt what becomes almost a phonetic representation of the dialect. I have chosen to compromise. Unless the character speaking is exceptionally broadly spoken I have retained the English spelling of any Scots word which resembles the English, leaving the reader to imagine accent or other variance. I hope that his may not offend the devotees of the Scottish language.

G.H.

ONE

'I'm not getting at you, Peter. You're the exception that more than proves the rule. But I'm getting fed up to the teeth with well-heeled city-types who come into the countryside for a bit of recreation and bring a taint of class-warfare into the few pursuits that make a rural life tolerable. Don't laugh, damn you!'

'Can't help it,' said Sir Peter Hay. 'Nobody's ever suggested that your favourite pursuit was the prerogative of the rich.' He looked at his friend with amusement.

The younger man refused to smile. 'Not any more,' he said. 'I'm a reformed character and without recourse to surgery. Come back to the point. Take shooting. It applies to other sports, but we'll stick to shooting. There's – what is it? – about nine hundred thousand shotgun users in the country, but because the papers are only interested in the doings of a wealthy minority, everybody believes that the whole scene's taken up with beaters and driven game and tweeds and Purdeys and whole mountains of the slain. And then whenever a question arises, and especially when somebody wants a cheap band-wagon to jump on, the cry goes up, "Rich man's sport, clobber it!" Only they disguise it behind a camouflage of other reasons and perpetuate a whole series of myths to justify themselves.'

'Just what you're doing too,' said Sir Peter. 'I always knew you were an inverted snob and you've just proved it.'

'How?' demanded Keith Calder. 'How have I?'

'You don't like the rich so you blame them for attacks on

your sport, closing your mind to the debt that wildlife owes to the big shooting estates.

'Anyway, Ray Grass was a far cry from your pet aversions. He'd rather have spent a day pottering about after the bunnies with a gun and a scruffy old spaniel than have spent it shooting his own driven pheasants. Of *course* he held some big shoots that figured in the glossies. Why wouldn't he? He had a big estate and all the money he could want. He might have been born to money, but he founded and built up one of the biggest chemicals companies in the world, and he was still chairman and managing director of it, and major shareholder. That sort of entertaining wasn't just expected of him, it was necessary. But I've been on one or two of those shoots, and Ray usually went along as a picker-up and worked a dog or two.'

Keith shrugged. 'All right. So he was one of us. Maybe I'd have liked him. That still doesn't impel me to blither off to the other side of Scotland to help clear up his estate.'

'I thought you did like him,' Sir Peter said simply. 'You spent half the evening discussing matchlocks and miquelets with him.' He leaned back against a dry-stone wall and smiled. The farmland patchwork of the Scottish borders reached away below them, and Sir Peter's pleasure in the early summer scene was neither increased nor diminished by the fact that most of it was his own. Close in front of them, Keith's spaniel and two of Sir Peter's many Labradors were enjoying an informal hunt through a plantation of young conifers. A blackcock took wing indignantly and Sir Peter lifted his gun.

'Bang!' he said. 'That beggar'll be back in season before very long. Does more damage in forestry than roe-deer.'

Keith brushed a cleg away from his face. 'After your Boxing Day shoot? Was that him? I never caught his name and he didn't let on that he had tuppence to rub together, though he had a damn good gun. Yes, I did like him. But the point is, I can't take time off whenever I want it.'

'You're taking it off now,' Sir Peter said.

'That's different.'

'Because you want it to be different?'

'Not at all,' Keith said with dignity. 'I spare myself half a Saturday occasionally and an hour or two of an evening, but if I take on anything else it'll have to come off the business. And I can't afford that.'

Sir Peter chuckled and shook his head, so that his tangled grey hair dripped shadows across his face. 'Don't tell me that the business isn't making money. You'll soon be so rich that other men will be complaining that you add to the myth that shooting's a rich man's sport.'

'Then why do I always seem to be scratching around to find the next ha'penny?'

'Because you plough it all back. I dare say that if you added up the value of all the shotguns you've got in the shop, and the fishing tackle and cartridges and other gear, let alone the antique guns that you try to avoid selling again, you'd find that you'd put by quite a wheen of money these last few years. Doesn't that young partner of yours tell you that? He is an accountant, after all.'

'Just as long as he keeps the tax-man off my back I don't have to listen to him,' Keith says. 'When he talks about money he's in another language.'

'Well, if you like to think that you're a pauper far be it from me to disabuse you. I'll just point out that what I'm asking you to do is to help settle up the estate of a very rich man. And the fees for that sort of work can be very fat indeed. They may not be up to what you could make skinning my friends over second-hand guns that you've bodged back into some sort of shape –'

'Here!'

'– but they should exceed your hourly rate for gunsmith work or coaching by a handsome margin. When a rich man dies, the vultures tend to move in. Well, it was with that in mind that I suggested that he make Ralph Enterkin the executor of his personal estate. But Ralph isn't going to work for sweeties – why should he? He's a damned good lawyer, and he's worth his hire on that sort of job.'

'Good luck to him,' Keith said. 'He won't need me.'

Sir Peter sighed. 'He can't value the best-class guns, nor a substantial collection of antique weapons; and he'll need expert and independant advice about the shooting on the estate.'

'The guns could be brought to me.'

The baronet dropped the barrels of his gun and squinted through the bores. 'All right,' he said, 'you force me to ask you a personal favour. I, personally, want your opinion.' He unfolded his long frame, stood up and brushed grass from his threadbare kilt.

'Opinion?' Keith stood up and whistled his dog. The spaniel came running, a big grin on her face.

Sir Peter called to his Labradors. They paid not the least attention. 'That makes three of you,' he said sadly. 'Yes, your opinion. You know how Ray Grass died?'

'I read something in the papers. Some kind of shooting accident?'

They started to move down the hill. Keith had to step out to match the baronet's stride. 'The fiscal's enquiry,' Sir Peter said, 'brought in that he slipped while climbing a fence with a loaded gun.'

'That's not how I remember him,' Keith said, frowning. 'I

10

noticed that he opened and emptied his gun before he'd even step over a stile. Very much by the book.'

'I thought so too. Of course, people do set themselves a lower standard when they're on their own – there's nobody else to endanger. But, to me, it just isn't the way he was.'

'Hell of a job to prove anything, without any witnesses.'

'Problems are for solving. You'll take it on, then?'

'Don't rush me,' Keith said. 'I'll have to see if I can get away.'

'You mean you'll have to see whether Molly'll let you off the lead?' The words were not said unkindly. The baronet's own Ladyship, when at home, was inclined to be possessive.

'Something like that,' Keith said.

'Shall we have a go at the rabbits on the Long Brae?'

'Let's do just that.'

Back at home, tired and contented, Keith found Briesland House open but empty. From a window, he could see his wife at work among the shrubs that took up much of the garden. It was their season and the colours blazed under the gentle sun. Molly's shape was changing and he thought, not for the only time, that in the bloom of her first pregnancy her dark looks were maturing into real beauty, serene and yet exciting. Already Molly was reluctant to go down on her knees. Instead, a spray container was slung over her shoulder and with its lance she was selecting weeds among the perennials for a quick mist of Paraquat.

Keith smiled. He made two long drinks, a strong whisky and a very weak gin-and-tonic, loaded them with ice and carried them out, carefully because of the spaniel pushing past his feet, to where two deckchairs and an iron table waited in the shade of a beech tree. 'Come and relax,' he said.

Molly came, smiling the smile that she kept for him alone.

She doomed one last dandelion with a hiss from her spray, then laid it down and flopped into one of the chairs and mopped her brow. 'It's a bit warm for gardening,' she said.

'Well, don't overdo it. We'd rather have weeds than a miscarriage, now that we've got this far. Now, listen.' Briefly, he outlined Sir Peter's proposition.

When he had finished Molly sat silent for a minute, absently scratching the head of the panting dog and looking down the valley to the town of Newton Lauder. She thought that they owed Sir Peter a thousand favours. 'You wouldn't want to lose the business and goodwill to somebody else,' she said at last. 'I see that. And if there was anything wrong about his death, I think you should help if you can. I remember him from Sir Peter's party. I liked him a lot. He spoke very nicely to me. And he was one of those people who like to laugh a lot – no, that's not quite right – who laugh a lot because they're happy.'

'You think I should do it? I've got a hell of a lot on.'

'You always have. But we've finished the decorating, and Janet and Wal can run the shop between them for a bit. What else have you got?'

'Several coaching sessions.'

'At the clay pigeons? Wallace can do that. He enjoys it. And he had the knack of teaching. What else?'

'Gundog classes.'

'I'll do those for you,' Molly offered, 'and I can deal with any correspondence about the antiques side of things if you leave everything tidy and labelled. Do you have any gun repairs that can't wait?'

'Nothing I couldn't polish off tomorrow if I got down to it. You could manage? I may have to be away for several days at a time.'

Although she could almost feel a second lump in her sto-

12

mach, Molly managed to laugh. 'With Mrs Jelks coming in for mornings, of course I can manage. Can you leave me the car, and Tanya for company?'

At the sound of her name, the spaniel squirmed in the grass.

'I shan't need the car. They're sending something plushy to fetch us.' Keith sounded impressed. He was still new to the ways of the rich, and the idea of sending a large car on a round journey of more then two hundred miles was foreign to him. 'You can keep Tanya if you promise me faithfully that you won't let her have any buns or potatoes to eat. And if Jack Waterhouse comes back about the Baker rifle, tell him that I'm not coming down another penny. You can be as rude as you like; I don't care if I never see him again. He's a rotten customer, and I think he's going off his chump.'

'All right. Keith . . .' Molly's momentary silence was filled by a thrush singing in the tree above. Molly had never been under any delusions about Keith. She had known him for a rake when she married him, had held him on a carefully loose rein, and had felt ready to explode with relief and joy when he had turned into an almost perfect husband. The leopard's spots, however, may fade but never disappear. There had been lapses. Molly was determined not to assume the ugliness of the jealous wife but . . . there were always buts.

'Keith,' she said, 'if I promise about Tanya, will you promise me something in return?'

'Yes, of course,' Keith said absently. 'What?'

Molly turned pink. Her vocal cords seemed to have turned into rhubarb. 'Promise me that if you can't look me in the eye and tell me truthfully that there's been nobody else you won't come back at all.' Keith, she was almost sure, had never lied to her.

Keith was taken aback. He honestly believed himself to be

quite the most faithful, loyal and considerate of husbands. Any trifling lapses from that ideal had been no more than the passing impulses of an affectionate nature — what he had once referred to as a "flash in the pants" — and anyway Molly knew nothing of them. 'You didn't have to say that,' he said reproachfully. 'Of course I promise. But I shouldn't have to. You knew that I'd been wild before you married me. You, more than anybody else, were part of my wildness. And now my reputation follows me around. I've only got to nod in the street to some fat old bag with a moustache and a wooden leg and the tongues are wagging again.'

Molly was feeling a little better. 'You can leave my relatives out of this,' she said.

'I'm a respectable businessman now, and happily married with it,' Keith persisted. 'And I want to stay that way. Is that good enough?'

'Quite good enough. And, Keith, if there is anything going on that shouldn't be . . .'

'Don't worry. I'll not get involved in anything rough. If I turn up something murky, the fuzz can deal with it or the lawyers.' He got up, drained his glass and stretched. 'I'd better go and clear my feet, if I'm taking time away.'

Molly waited anxiously. Their private convention demanded that Keith make some little joke, just to show that his feelings had not been hurt. The moment dragged out. Either Keith was offended, Molly thought, or he could not think of a joke. She held her breath. Even the thrush was silent.

'Yuck!' Keith said suddenly. 'That's the last time I drink Champagne out of *your* slipper.'

'It was giving me foot-rot anyway,' Molly said happily.

14

TWO

At an uncomfortably early hour of the Monday morning a Rolls Royce the colour of darkish coffee – upholstered, aptly enough, in cream – collected Keith and his luggage from the door of Briesland House. He was hardly seated before the uniformed chauffeur, in his cell beyond the glass screen, made some gentle passes and the car oozed silently over the uneven approach-road where Keith's own car was wont to bounce and rattle.

Ralph Enterkin was already enthroned beside him on the back seat. Keith thought that he had come to know the solicitor well over the years, and he was surprised to find a young, black Labrador curled on the car's floor, its chin resting proprietorially on Mr Enterkin's instep. Keith had never taken the corpulent little man for a gun-dog enthusiast, his pleasures seeming to run more towards good food and wines, his own voice and his bed – the last, Keith gathered, not always in the solitary state which his bachelor status demanded.

'Your dog?' Keith asked.

'He seems to think so, or possibly *vice versa*. Name of Brutus. Bequeathed to me by a nephew who emigrated last month to some rabies-infested hole. A delightful character, but demanding. He takes me for walks,' Mr Enterkin said plaintively. 'However, I dare say that the exercise is beneficial. I think I was in danger of putting on a little weight.' He patted his protuberant stomach.

'Does he come from working stock, or is he for showing?'

'I haven't the faintest idea. Does it matter?'

'Not if you don't want to work him.'

'My nephew said something about training him for field trials.' The solicitor looked out of the window at the country-side sliding by. 'What splendid weather for being conveyed opulently over the moors towards a fat fee at the other end.'

'Can you leave your practice for days at a time?' Keith asked. Mr Enterkin was a one-man firm.

'Bless you, my boy,' the solicitor said, chuckling, 'I could probably leave it for years without anyone noticing. The practice of law is largely common sense obscured by jargon. Learn the language and it's all written down somewhere. Nine-tenths of my work is conveyancing and the invaluable Miss Wilks does practically all of it. I live in comfortably suspended animation, rousing myself only when one of my more interesting clients is trapped *in flagrante delicto,* or gets his head caught in a breathalyser. The rest of the working day I spend browsing through my legal tomes which, for those who can read them, contain more and better tales of quite astonishing humour and not a little salacity than you would ever find on the shelves in the public library. Every extraordinary deed brings its perpetrator to court in the end. And the tales happen to be true, or as true as the rules of evidence will permit.'

He fell silent. Keith had a momentary mental picture of the solicitor sitting between meals in his dusty sanctum and poring through his books of law, bored and lonely. He brushed the vision aside. Mr Enterkin was the most gregarious of men.

'You know why you're coming along?' Enterkin asked.

'I'm along to make an offer for any good antique guns,' Keith said.

The solicitor sighed. 'I might have remembered your propensity for picking nits where no nits exist. Did Sir Peter tell you why I wanted you along?'

'Yes. Value the guns, do any necessary repairs, advise on the shooting and confirm that there was nothing wrong with the death. Right?'

'You could put it like that. You'd not be very near the mark, but you could. Never mind. All will be revealed to you in the fullness of time. You met the late Mr Grass. What did you think of him?'

'I liked him,' Keith said, 'I think because he radiated good humour. He seemed to enjoy life and laughter. If I'd realised that he was rolling in it I might have liked him even more.'

'You like people for their money?'

'I might have respected him for staying warm and human in spite of it,' Keith said. 'How comfortable was he?'

'Comfortable?' Enterkin gave a snort of laughter. 'That's a term you might use of a grocer's widow. It doesn't begin to apply. Grass was right in there with the Duke of Westminster and the oil-rig workers. Pop stars took off their Stetsons when he went by. His grandfather started the family fortune with property. His father stayed with property and enlarged it. Then Grass came along and built up a struggling firm that had been one of his father's side-interests into a booming multinational group of companies that he still owned the lion's share of. And he had a thousand other irons in the fire. He was an inspired organiser. He'd a genius for picking the right advisers, setting up the perfect *modus operandi* and then leaving the right men to get on with it. And he managed to keep a lot of his loot by applying the same principles to his accountancy.'

Keith made a mental note of those words of wisdom. The late Mr Grass's example was worth following. 'No wonder he could afford to laugh.'

The solicitor's round but usually goodhumoured face developed a petulant scowl. 'He had a sense of humour, but it had failed to develop after about the fourth form at school. I'm told that he kept it under strict control in the course of his business dealings but . . . What, Keith, is your own attitude to death?'

Keith blinked. 'The question seems to be what you'd probably call a *non sequitur*,' he said.

Enterkin's scowl deepened. 'It isn't and I wouldn't and answer it anyway,' he snapped.

'If I can't take it with me, I'm not going to go.'

'There you are,' Enterkin said. 'There you are. If you can't run away from it, laugh at it. And you can only run away just so far from death. When it came down to working on his will, Grass seemed to unleash a long-repressed streak of schoolboy humour. I managed to veto some of his wilder fantasies, and even so I think he'd have taken his business elsewhere if I hadn't been doing a superlative job on the new trust,' Mr Enterkin said modestly.

Keith had no intention of letting the solicitor get launched on the subject of his own legal genius. 'Peter seemed to think that there might have been something wrong with his death,' he said. 'Disbelieving an accident because the man was usually careful doesn't give much to go on. Was there anything else?'

Mr Enterkin, when in pensive mood, had a habit of protruding his lips like a child sucking on a straw, and he did it now. The grimace reminded Keith of an aggressive tropical fish. 'I went through for the fatal accident enquiry. No evidence was brought out that indicated anything other than an accident. I got the feeling that the sheriff and the procurator fiscal and the chief constable had all made up their minds that it was an accident and that they wanted to conclude the matter without scandal or delay.'

'Nobody was going to make waves?'

'That's what I *said*. One witness, a young officer who had

been first on the scene and who appeared to know some-thing about shotguns, began to draw attention to some discrepant factor, but he was instantly suppressed. What do you suppose it might have been?'

Keith almost imitated Mr Enterkin's grimace – it was a catching habit. 'You don't get much ballistic evidence with a shotgun,' he said. 'Even so, there might ber pointers. I take it that he wasn't carrying a hammer-gun?'

'I'm sure I couldn't say. They mentioned a maker's name which reminded me, for some reason, of war-time. But not as the name of a gun.'

'When I met him,' Keith said, 'he was carrying a Churchill Premier.'

'That was it.'

'A gun of that quality would have intercepting sears, sort of second line of defence to catch the internal hammers if the trigger-sears get jolted off. If they were still in working order, no way should a gun like that go off for a fall. I'd better take a look inside when we get our hands on it. Was there nothing else?'

'Nothing. The whole thing was very quick and cursory, once they had at long last established his identity. Talk about one law for the rich and another for the poor!' Mr Enterkin said disgustedly. 'Quite apart from the infamous Legal Aid Scheme, which decrees that only a poor man should ever go to law. If the body had been that of a teenage, black, preg-nant, Lesbian terrorist – which characteristics are not as incompatible as some might think – a dozen civil rights organisations would have been screaming for enquiry before a jury; but a rich man's death can be swept under the carpet without a voice being raised. The rich, it seems, are fair game.'

'Get me a look at the gun, and we'll see if we can raise

some voices,' Keith said. 'Did Grass have any enemies?'

A gleam of satisfaction showed in Enterkin's eyes. As Sir Peter had suggested, Keith had only to be started on the trail and his hunter's instinct would take over. 'No enemies that I know of, although a man with that kind of Puckish humour and the money to indulge it must have annoyed a few people in his time. And you don't act as a money-magnet for thirty years without somebody hating you. He didn't grind the faces of widows and orphans much. He could grind the faces of rival corporations, but I don't see the directors of I.C.I. putting out a contract on him.'

'Well then, who's better off for his death? Apart from yourself, of course.'

Enterkin accepted the slur without animus. 'I'd have been the very last to wish him dead,' he said. 'A rich man who changed his personal bequests every few minutes was almost the perfect client. We should have bred from him while we had the chance. Now all I've got to look forward to is the fee for executing the damned will. And that, believe you me, is going to be hard work. I'll tell you this much. He had no near kin. He made provision for his business interests to go fully public, which should both ensure their survival and inflate his pre-tax estate enormously. Most of the estate goes into a trust, and I can't think of anybody who would have any motive to bump him off for that. The rest is dribbled away in personal bequests, and it's to be admitted that some of those are fairly handsome.'

They were silent, each busy with his own thoughts, until the big car was sliding through Peebles. The sight of the Peebles Hydro Hotel reminded Keith of something. 'Are we staying at Whinkirk House?'

'I've booked us into the Falcon Inn for the moment,' Enterkin said. 'As an executor, I've stayed in bereaved houses

20

before. The staff goes to pot, and if there's a bottle of decent wine in the cellar the relatives are scrambling for it.'

'But if we stay at a nearby five-star hotel and charge it to the estate, that's legitimate?'

'Perfectly.'

'And is the Falcon Inn five-star?'

'I doubt if it could survive the shock of being granted the tiniest meteorite. Its ancient walls would crumble. But it used to house the overflow of Grass's guests, so the hospitality should meet even my lofty standards.'

'I take it,' Keith said, 'that this car comes up to your standards?'

'This,' Mr Enterkin admitted, 'is what I would call a gentlemanly way to travel.' He leaned forward and touched a button in a console. Jazz in stereo pulsed softly around them. 'Telephone, television, tape-recorder, you name it. He liked to use the car as his office extension, do his homework on his way to a meeting, action it on the way home and then be free to forget it.' He stretched comfortably and looked out of the window. 'We could do with more days like this. But if we will live almost exactly the same distance from the Equator as is Cape Horn we must accept what we get in the knowledge that we asked for it. It's only the Gulf Stream that keeps this country habitable, and the Americans would put a meter on that if they could.'

Keith had been musing while Mr Enterkin rambled on. 'It must be one hell of a temptation,' he said. 'I mean, if you've got all the money in the world and nobody to leave it to. I suppose you could leave a packet to the minister's favourite charity, provided that he preached a sermon while wearing horns and a forked tail?'

'You could,' Mr Enterkin said, 'if your sense of humour was as puerile as that of my late client. I had to dissuade him from several pranks of that nature, and about one or two he remained adamant.'

'Is that what you fell out about?'

'Not exactly, no.' Enterkin sighed. 'He wanted to specify the epitaph to be carved on his gravestone.'

'Can somebody do that?' Keith asked. The chance to commemorate some of his own achievements seemed almost irresistable.

'Within reason, yes. If your proudest moment were the bedding of some great lady – which may indeed be the case – that would never be acceptable. But if you wished to have recorded your prowess at dominoes, or the fact that you once killed an elephant with your bare hands, your executor would no doubt carry out your wishes. Mr Grass, however, explained to me with the utmost seriousness that he took more pride in his own culinary ability than in all his business achievements. In particular, he said, he was proud of his game soup – which I must admit I had sampled and found excellent. And,' Mr Enterkin said indignantly, 'I damned nearly fell for it.'

'Fell for what? A talent for cookery seems harmless enough.'

'That's what I thought at the time. The penny only dropped when I heard a chef using the same words about a certain cut of venison. But for that I should have found myself bound, and by a will of my own drafting, to have had the words carved on his tombstone. The appalling implica-tions had quite passed me by, largely because he was still, at the time, extant. I mean such a phrase may be used of last night's hostess without offence. Applied to a deceased, the words acquire quite a different connotation.'

'*What* words?'

'The words, "He made excellent soup". And don't *laugh*

like that,' Mr Enterkin said irritably.

They fell silent. Keith was wondering which gun from his personal collection would be a sufficient legacy to induce his brother-in-law to attend his, Keith's, funeral wearing a pair of suitably apologetic sandwich-boards. He would have been astonished to learn that Mr Enterkin was enjoying a vision of his own obsequies, attended by Keith in the role and costume of a harem eunuch.

THREE

Although the big car seemed to be drifting along at little more than walking-speed, they reached the village of Whinkirk with an hour to spare before lunch. So, while Keith went on to the inn, Mr Enterkin dropped off at the manse.

The Reverend Alec Foster was a silver-haired, silver-tongued widower of around sixty, with a face so calm and mild that Enterkin thought him beyond all passion.

Mr Enterkin found himself mistaken.

'I'll be damned if I do it,' said the minister. 'Literally, I mean.'

'Not according to the presbytery clerk,' Enterkin said. 'It was checked with him when the will was written.'

The minister almost snarled. 'Sometimes it seems to me that that man is so with-it that you'd think he invented it. Whatever it is. But don't quote me. Anyway, Enterkin, I won't do it.'

'If you don't, then bang goes your fifty thousand quid for the restoration fund,' Enterkin pointed out. 'Not literally bang. It goes to the local hunt, not towards shooting. And knowing your aversion . . .'

'Preposterous!' the older man broke in. He was too gentle to shout and thump the table, but his voice was quivering with the effort required to restrain himself. 'Apparently I'm expected to officiate at a – a sort of fancy-dress burial service scripted by the deceased himself.'

'Of course, it can only be a memorial service,' Enterkin said. 'He was buried some weeks ago. But in view of the diffi-

24

culty over identification, and the adjournment of the fiscal's enquiry, the courts have only just allowed the will to be proved.'

'Can't the conditions be upset? Not the bequests but the conditions? The man was a notorious lunatic.'

'I'm afraid not. It was very carefully worded in accordance with his own instructions. If anyone seeks to challenge the will, the alternative bequests prevail; and each is calculated to be as undesirable as possible to the original legatee.'

'The man was mad!'

'I'd like to be able to agree with you, Mr Foster. But in point of fact and to be strictly fair, he was no more than a man with money and no relatives, and who liked a good . . . well, I believe belly-laugh is the contemporary expression. I think that he wanted to make it the kind of occasion that he himself would have enjoyed. And, believe me, it could have been much worse. I dissuaded him from incorporating a group into the service.'

'Group?'

'A pop group. *Pretty Faeces,* I believe they call themselves. Some would tell you that they are the new culture.'

'The clerk to the presbytery is one of them. But, while I must bow to his edicts, something inside me cries out that the whole thing is verging on heresy.'

Enterkin sighed and began picking up his papers. It seemed to him that he was doomed to have variants of the same conversation with half a hundred other legatees. 'Well,' he said, 'we all have our cross to bear, if I may borrow the metaphor. To me falls the task of explaining to each beneficiary in turn the conditions of his or her inheritance.'

The minister, who was plainly preoccupied with his own problems, seemed unimpressed. 'A small professional service, and doubtless more than adequately remunerated.'

'I wish I thought so. I have a suspicion that my fee will be hard-earned. I myself gave up a legacy and spared you further agony thereby.'

The minister was not a malicious man, but misery loves company. 'Tell me,' he said.

'Mr Grass wanted to leave his Rolls Royce to the composer of the best graveside eulogy. It was to be in the form of a Limerick, and in return for being sole judge of merit I was also to figure among the lesser legatees.'

The minister sat up straight. Fine motor-cars were the only worldly goods to which he gave even passing respect, and his Vauxhall was unlikely to pass its next M.O.T. test. 'Rolls Royce?' he said. 'The Camargue?'

'I – er – I think so. I persuaded him to abandon the idea.'

The minister stopped himself from saying, 'What did you do that for?' Instead, he sighed. He could surely have afforded the petrol to take him the hundred yards or so between the manse and the church a few times each week. 'I suppose that I'll just have to do it,' he said. 'Duty compels me to sink my own feelings and put a new roof on the kirk. If the present roof were less dilapidated or the building less beautiful . . . But you can take it that I'll meet the condition.'

Enterkin coughed. 'We'll have another discussion after I've seen the other legatees. You see, some of the conditions attaching to the other legacies also bear upon the – er – service.'

'How do you mean?'

Enterkin failed to meet the minister's eye. 'Oh, just that some of the legacies have conditions concerning attendance at the service. Behaviour, or – er – dress and so on. If they're all accepted . . . Of course, I can't discuss details with you yet.'

'Of course not,' said the minister, without quite understanding why.

'After all, I'm sure you wouldn't turn away a hippy from your doors, just because of the garb,' Enterkin said nervously. 'Well, I must be going.'

'I'll see you out.'

At the front door, they paused and shook hands. 'I suppose the body really was your client's,' the minister said suddenly.

'The police, the sheriff and the Court of Session have all pronounced themselves satisfied.'

'I suppose so. With anyone else, I would accept their judgement. But it would be so much in keeping with his character to arrange his own funeral with a mind to being present himself, perhaps to make a dramatic appearance at the end of it.'

Enterkin gave the matter serious consideration. 'I think you can forget that idea,' he said. 'Mr Grass was a shrewd man. He would have known that by the time that he leaped from the coffin, or whatever else you think that he had in mind, most of his business interests would have passed irrecoverably into other hands. I don't think he'd have risked that.'

The Reverend Mr Foster returned to his study. He looked out at his sunlit garden. It was the perfect time of year and the colours seemed to dance in the bright light, but for once it brought him no comfort. He would dearly have loved a chance to own the great car, even for a few months before selling it to aid his beloved church.

His lips moved, and the casual observer might have believed the minister to be deep in prayer. The less casual observer, using his ears, might have discovered otherwise.

'Raymond De Basily Grass,' the minister murmured, 'Is no longer with us, alas!'

There was a protracted pause.

'Dear Lord,' he muttered at last, 'the truth is as dear to you as to me. You alone might forgive me if I suggested that he

27

was sometimes a pain in the . . . Aye, just so.'

Putting aside such unworthy thoughts, Mr Foster set himself to prepare his next sermon. He chose Covetousness as his subject, and he brought thereto more sympathy and understanding than was his custom.

At the gate, Mr Enterkin looked around and called 'Brutus!'

Brutus came round the corner of the manse, looking guilty. Patiently, he endured a short scolding for wandering off when told to stay, and he followed at heel all the way to the Falcon Inn.

Mr Enterkin was deep in thought.

Brutus was also thinking, in the intuitive, sense-oriented manner of a dog. From the thousand scents around the manse he could, if gifted with speech, have given his master a great deal of information about the minister and his household. But his uppermost thought was that the manse dustbin had been very poor foraging.

The Falcon Inn came very close to Keith's ideal of the perfect pub, being cool, calm and quiet. There was no juke-box to please one customer and annoy a dozen. The bedrooms might have been considered Spartan by Raymond Grass's guests, but they were just what Keith was used to and there was not the least trace of damp. His bed, Keith noticed automatically, was silent. Not that he had any intentions which might cause springs to jangle in the night, but habit died hard.

He unpacked his gear, admired the view from his window over the Solway Firth, pottered about in the bathroom and then made his way down to explore the inn. The public bar was crowded with strangers and housed a noisy darts match, but next door Keith found a private bar, empty but for a barmaid busily polishing glasses. Keith summed her up as cuddlesome, and left it at that.

He carried his pint to a table. The beer was excellent, from a small, local brewery, but Keith was only vaguely aware of it. He stared, unseeing, at a ribald sporting print and thought about guns. How could a gun like the Churchill go off by being dropped? He must get hold of the gun and take a look at the works. Rust or grit in the mechanism could have held back the intercepting sear. Of course, even a rich man might leave his best gun at home and carry an inexpensive import, if he were going where it might be damaged. Near salt water, for instance, or agricultural chemicals.

It might be illuminating to find out whether the police had studied the pellets of shot. Were they compatible with the expended cartridge-case? If so, did the marks of firing-pin and extractor match Mr Grass's gun?

The arrival of Brutus, greeting him as a long-lost friend, blew Keith's train of thought to tatters. Mr Enterkin was standing at the bar. Keith fussed with the dog until the solicitor brought his sherry across and sat down.

'Lunch,' he said, 'and then I think we'll go and visit a general.' The barmaid was called through to the other bar. 'What a charming young woman that is, to be sure.'

'Not so young,' Keith said. 'And she's married.' Keith noticed wedding rings.

So also did Mr Enterkin. 'Widowed,' he said. 'I asked. And from my standpoint she is a mere child. But a child with a magnificent figure.'

'You're turning into a dirty old man.'

'Thank you,' Mr Enterkin said, 'but I don't deserve it.'

'You used to have a comfortable arrangement with a lady nearer home.'

'It became somewhat less comfortable last year, and was

29

terminated by mutual agreement. That young woman,' Mr
Enterkin said thoughtfully, 'carries her bosom as if she were
proud of it, which is a rare change these days. A thoroughly
womanly woman,' he added, 'except that she doesn't talk all
the time. Just deals with the subject and then is content with
silence.'

'She probably couldn't get a word in edgeways,' Keith said.
'Anyway, you should have put all that sort of thing behind
you by now.'

'The devil may sleep, my boy, but he never dies. Sometimes he sleeps very lightly.' Mr Enterkin craned his neck to
inspect himself in the mirror behind the bar.

'I don't recognise the accent. Where does she come from?'

'West country.'

Keith frowned. 'We're about as far west as you can get.'

'Devon or Somerset, you ignorant youth.' But Mr
Enterkin's mind was not behind the rebuke. He had spent
part of the war near Taunton, and he was remembering with
nostalgia a rich countryside, farmhouse teas and friendship
easily given.

Although they lunched separately, the men and the dog,
they lunched similarly. The inn was unpretentious, with a
small dining room in which the landlord, a barrel-shaped
ex-boxer named Harvey Brown, served them with a steak pie
which made Mr Enterkin croon with pleasure. In the yard
behind the inn Mrs Brown, who among other duties acted as
principal cook, served the steak pie to Brutus. She had
examined the tins of dog-meat which Mr Enterkin had provided, and had set them aside for the next visiting tramp.

FOUR

The village comprised a number of houses and cottages, a
few shops, the inn and two insignificant public houses, and a
church. The buildings were of a variety of ages and styles,
and they had grown, mingled haphazardly with unnumbered
large trees, along and around a single street which was also
the road from nowhere in particular to somewhere
unimportant and so carried no traffic other than the purely
local and mainly agricultural.

At the far end of the village and up a short lane they found
a large Victorian house surrounded by rhododendrons. With
the sun shining on the old stone, the bushes in bloom and
backed by the trees with which the area was so well
endowed, it looked pleasant enough; but Keith thought that
it might be a depressing sort of dump in mid-winter.

General Springburn was a large man. Although well on in
his sixties he still showed a bursting vitality that Keith found
rather overpowering. He met them at the door and bade
them enter, in a voice which made Brutus squat down. 'Bring
the dog in,' he roared. 'Dogs welcome in this house. Mine're
shut up in back. Come into gunroom.'

The general had twinkling eyes yet a curiously expression-
less face. Later, they were to appreciate that he had attained
high rank early in life. Many years spent setting an example,
keeping a stiff upper lip, showing the flag and standing no
nonsense had set on him a stiff outer crust through which a
schoolboyish sense of humour sometime managed to escape.
This, Keith came to think, might have been the attraction

31

between the general and Raymond Grass – two Peter Pans imprisoned in elderly and respectable gentlemen.

The gunroom was a large room at the back of the house, looking onto a heavily overgrown garden. A long gunrack held several shotguns and a rifle, and on the wall above was hung a modest collection of flintlocks and early percussion guns. Keith started to look at them but something half-registered was calling his attention. Two oval patches on the walls showed signs of repair, one of them recent. Nearby, the woodwork of the window seemed to have suffered attack by beetles. Keith inferred that his years of service had failed to inculcate in the general a proper respect for firearms, or else that familiarity had bred contempt.

Brutus lay down under the big table that filled the centre of the room. He was puzzled and therefore nervous. The general would be the wrong person to disobey. Yet, from their scents, the general's dogs were fat and lazy.

'Had a letter about you,' the general boomed. He picked up the barrels of a twelve-bore. 'Mind if I finish? You're the legal eagle, right? Come to tell me about Grass's will?'

'That's right,' Enterkin said. 'And Mr Calder is advising me about guns and shooting matters.'

'Know him,' said the general. He shook Keith's hand, violently. 'Heard you speak. Club meeting. Cartridges and patterns. Spoke well. Didn't agree with it all. Long as it goes bang and bird comes down, don't need all that science.' He swung back to Enterkin. 'Well?'

The lawyer opened his case and took out a paper. He knew the terms of the will by heart, but a paper to scrutinise saved him from having to meet the eyes of the legatees. In this instance it also saved him from watching the barrels of the shotgun, which more often than not seemed to be pointing at himself.

'You're mentioned more than once in the will,' he said. 'You must have known him well.'

'Very well. Liked him. Usually. Sense of humour. Liked that. Sometimes let it run away with him of course.'

'Firstly, this house.'

'Lease runs out soon.'

'Quite so. The will provides that you can occupy it for your lifetime, for a peppercorn rent.'

The general blew out his breath. 'Thank God! Been worried. But . . . I understand . . . conditions?'

'Not in this instance.'

The general lit up. 'Well, bless him and may he rest in peace! Best news you could have brought me. Like a drink?'

'Not just now, thank you,' Mr Enterkin said. Keith shook his head.

'Sensible chaps. Well, anything else? You said . . .'

'Yes.' Enterkin rattled his papers. 'You understand that the other bequests have conditions attached to them?'

'Oh. Yes. Heard about those conditions.' The general slammed the gun into the rack and took another out. 'You'd better tell me the worst. No, hang on a minute. Hear my daughter.' He threw open the door. 'Pru? Come in here a minute. This is the lawyer chap and his pal. Says I can stay on in the house.'

The general's daughter was a pleasant-looking woman in her thirties, dressed in sensible but hot tweeds. 'I'm glad for you, Dad. Although this house is too big for you. Do put that thing down. I brought the twins over. They're playing outside.' She nodded and smiled to Mr Enterkin and to Keith.

'It isn't loaded.' The general mounted the gun in the direction of the window. 'Want to stay here. Brought up in this house. Looked forward to settling down here. Hope to die here. Not just yet. Well, let's get the rest of the news and then we can have our walk.'

'You're not bringing that thing on our walk, are you?'

'Always ask that. Always am. Why ever not?'

'I'm just thinking about the children,' Pru said.

'Tell them not to come fluttering out of the tree-tops. I'm after pigeon, dammit.'

Mr Enterkin recaptured their attention with a determined flutter of papers. 'In token of the shooting that you and he had together, the will asks you to fire a salute over the grave. In return, you are bequeathed one of his antique guns, and a choice of any two others.'

The general's eyes gleamed. He drew himself up and tucked the gun under his arm. His daughter pushed the muzzles away from her body. 'It isn't loaded. By George! Something, that is! Couldn't've pleased me more. Better than anything I have here. Need a bit of restoration here or there, some of 'em, though.'

'Dad loves his old guns and things,' Pru said indulgently. 'If he had a tail, he'd wag it.'

'Am wagging, damn it. Which particular one did he leave me?'

Enterkin looked at his papers. 'It's referred to as a "Roman Candle". Could that be a typing error?'

'No. Right enough,' said the general. 'Splendid! Fine piece. Bit of history.' He resumed mounting his gun.

'That's the gun you're to fire the salute with.'

'*What?*' The general fumbled and hit himself on the ear with the butt of his gun. 'That . . . that *contraption*!'

'But Dad, you just said . . .'

'Nemmind what I just said. Facing angry mob, might be glad of it. Not in cold blood. Too easy lose some fingers.'

'Well, you don't have to do it if you don't want to,' Pru pointed out.

'Oh, suppose I'll do it.' The old soldier drew himself up. 'For that gun, the Manton and the snaphaunce . . .' He scratched the back of his neck with the muzzles of the shotgun. Not for the first time, Mr Enterkin was struck by the uncanny accuracy with which the late Mr Grass had predicted the inducement required for acceptance of his less acceptable conditions. 'But, don't know why he had to insist on that,' the general went on plaintively. 'Dammit, thought we were friends!'

'You did shoot him once, Dad,' Pru reminded him.

'Didn't exactly *shoot* him. Peppered him. Accidental.' The general thumped the butt of his gun down on the floor. 'Anyway, paid me back for that. By God he did!'

'What happened?' Keith asked, giving way to his curiosity.

The general gave a snort which, in earlier days, would have stopped a batallion in its tracks, and gestured with his gun at the chest of drawers beside the gun-rack. 'Load my own cartridges. Keep them loose in top two drawers. Next drawer for empties. Grass had some special cartridges loaded. Mixed them among mine. First time out, important shoot, wanted to make good impression. Damned embarrassing.' Lost for words, he mounted his gun and swung. Keith ducked out of the way.

Pru chuckled, not without a certain malicious pleasure. 'There wasn't any shot in them. Just a little balloon of soap or something. When Dad fired one, he filled the air with little coloured bubbles.'

Mr Enterkin did not appreciate the true awfulness of the revenge, but Keith was hard put to it not to laugh. He blew his nose hurriedly.

The general flushed. 'Damned embarrassing,' he repeated. 'Just been confined to house, did a big reloading, two thousand or more. Mixed them right through the lot. Think

I've got rid of the last of 'em now. Still finding them up to last month.' He mounted the gun again and swung through a fly that was tracking across the ceiling.

'Well, he hasn't done badly by you,' Pru said. 'You can earn your toys, and stay on in this house. Although you know you'd be welcome to a home with us.'

'Fair enough, Pru, fair enough. But as long as I'm fit, and can pay the rates. And the heating,' the general added gloomily.

'There is one last bequest,' Enterkin said. 'It figures also in the new deed of trust for the Whinkirk Estate. You are given permission to shoot vermin, including rabbit and wood-pigeon, on the estate, and you may attend and host the first pheasant-shoot of each season. The upkeep of the shooting has been provided for.'

'By George!' the general said again. Had his daughter not been present he might have called on someone rather higher in the celestial hierarchy. 'Now, that really is something!'

'Hold on a minute, Dad,' said Pru. 'Wait and see what strings are tied to it before you start the singing and dancing bit. It's all a bit too like one of those classical stories in which the gods give somebody his heart's desire in such a way that it doesn't do him a bit of good. Typical of that man Grass, of course. I can just imagine him pulling out the draft will on a dull evening and thinking to himself, "Who have I got it in for today, and what shall I make him do?" '

'All right, girl, all right. Don't go on like your mother used to.' He looked at Enterkin. 'Conditions?'

Enterkin coughed and fidgeted with his papers. Even in his ignorance he could see that this condition was going to be unpopular. 'The only condition is that you never shoot there

– take game or vermin, it says – except wearing a white coat. "Or similar white outer clothing". At least that allows you . . .'

The general dropped his gun, stooped over the table and put his head in his hands. 'The best bit of shooting in fifty miles and I have to stand out like a bloody snowman,' he mourned. 'Nothing that I've done deserves that.'

'I suppose he wanted to make sure that everyone else could see you,' Pru said bluntly.

'Can't think why,' the general said through his fingers.

'Because you're so careless. Frankly, Dad, when you're out with a gun I'll be only too happy to know that I can see you coming.'

'You don't know anything about it.'

'I know what everyone says.'

The general straightened up and squared his shoulders. He feared no man, but his daughter was something else. His shoulders drooped again. 'Not true,' he muttered. 'One or two isolated incidents. The odd near-miss. Happen to anybody.'

'But they didn't happen to anybody. They happened to you. I'm only surprised that it wasn't you who had the accident. Or killed somebody else. I suppose,' Pru added reflectively, 'that isn't what happened.'

'What?' the general demanded.

'That you shot him accidentally, and rigged it to look as if he'd had his own accident.'

General Springburn glowered horribly, which seemed to bother his daughter not at all. 'Good God!' he burst out. 'You're as bad as your mother for thinking the worst. I never saw him that day until after he was dead. I spotted Winter bending over him and went to see if I could help. Signs were clear enough to see. Climbing fence, slipped, dropped gun, gun went off. Shouldn't climb fence with loaded gun, but seen him do it before. Not often, but Homer can nod, eh?'

'How was he lying?' Keith asked.

'On back. One foot hooked in fence. Gun down the slope, other side. There you have it. Nutshell.'

Keith nodded. In a nutshell was exactly how he had it.

'His head and hands got the worst of it,' Pru said, 'as if he'd seen it coming and was trying to protect his face. That's why it took so long to obtain – what do they call it? – legal presumption of death or something. There was a lot of gossip in the village. There was a rumour that the police weren't being open about the evidence. People began to wonder whether the body was really his. Elaborate hoaxes were just his scene, and money stopped mattering to him in the last few years.'

Keith was slightly shocked. 'Surely,' he said, 'he'd have drawn the line at messing about with a dead body?'

'Don't know,' said the general. 'Knew him all his life. Wild boy. High-spirited. Seemed to settle down. Seemed to be getting wilder again after he made his pile. Didn't care. Owned small company making records, cassettes and things. Put out casette, *Music for the Motorway.* Doctored. Super-imposed noises. Big-end going. Overtaking police-car. Horns. Brakes. Voices. Garages did boom business. Verges littered with cars. Bloody dangerous. Gave money back and paid some damages, but couldn't see broken-down car without bursting out laughing. Quite blind to consequences. Apart from that, brilliant businessman and damn good landowner. English squire rather than Scottish laird.'

'Complete with *droit de seigneur,* from what one hears,' said his daughter.

'Wouldn't say that. Liked the girls, though. Never married. Well, with his money . . .'

Pru sniffed. 'He managed to get sued for breach of

promise, which I didn't think happened any more.'

'Years ago,' said the general. 'His own fault. Shouldn't have mentioned marriage in the first place. Shouldn't have kissed her in the second place.' The general paused and looked around. There was an unholy gleam in his eye. 'Should have stuck to the first place,' he added.

That was when Keith realised that the general was not quite the innocent old fool that he pretended to be.

There was a moment of shocked silence.

The general wandered to the open window. He mounted his gun, drew bead on a passing sparrow and blew it to shreds.

FIVE

General Springburn did not carry his gun that day. He seemed to feel naked without it, but the entire company was united against him. Even Mr Enterkin seemed to realise that he had just witnessed a startling exhibition of carelessness with a gun. As for Pru, this fresh reminder of her sire's irresponsibility made her adamant, and she hammered home her embargo by suggesting that perhaps they should call round and see whether any of the village shops had a white macintosh on offer. Or perhaps, in view of the weather, an umpire's white coat?

The three men followed her out quietly.

'Where now?' the general asked. He sounded, for him, subdued.

Enterkin looked at his watch. 'We're not expected at Whinkirk House until tomorrow. If the gamekeeper's handy – Colin Winter, isn't it? – we might just see him.'

'Going that way. Take you there.'

Pru's twin girls led the way with their mother in attendance. The men dropped back as far as they dared. Brutus stayed close to heel of his own volition as the general's two fat cockers romped around him, and he thought superior thoughts about them.

The general had been brooding. 'Always had permission from individual farmers,' he said. 'Must white coat start now? Or could I wear something else over it?'

Mr Enterkin was prepared to compromise, but he intercepted a glare from Keith – the one person present who

40

appreciated the mortal nature of the general's sin – and stood firm. The general walked on in a silence broken only by occasional murmurs of "White coat!" or "Little coloured bubbles!"

Keith took pity on him at last. 'Think of the shooting parties you can give,' he suggested. 'You don't have to shoot when you're the host, so you can wear what you like. Plan your invitations properly and you'll be sure of an invitation for every other Saturday in the season.'

'True,' the general said, brightening.

'That may have been what Raymond Grass had in mind. He could be very subtle,' Mr Enterkin pointed out. 'Perhaps this was his way of providing you with plenty of shooting, but not around here.'

The general seemed to hesitate over whether or not to take offence at the clumsy words but to decide against it. He might not like the conditions, but he could hardly cavil at the legacies.

They had left the village by a way that had started as a lane but was no longer pretending to be more than a track between fields. Now that they had emerged from the canopy of trees, Keith at last got a view of the estate, and he was impressed. It was farmed, and farmed well; but for at least a generation there had been a landlord who had not been driven by economic pressures to sacrifice the countryside on the altar of "prairie farming". Hedges rather than fences separated the fields. Long strips of woodland had been preserved, hedged against cattle, thinned for daylight and heavily undergrown. Every odd corner of the fields which might otherwise have been wasted was planted with cover. Keith got the impression of an estate managed as a balance of the interests of farming, shooting and wildlife. A cock pheasant strutted across the track, paying them little attention in the knowledge that he was safe at that season; but a pair of woodpigeon swerved as the general lifted his stick. The season for bird-song was almost past, but Keith was aware of more song-birds than he had seen at any one time since his boyhood.

The general sidled up against Keith, almost pushing him off the path. 'Nobody's going to make you wear a white coat around here?' he suggested, in a muted roar.

'I don't suppose so,' Keith said. 'But I haven't brought a gun.'

'Lend you a gun. Not long enough in neck and arms for any of mine. Wife had a sixteen-bore Sarasqueta, should fit you. Just 'til you get your own gun through. Call in tomorrow.'

Keith thanked him, while wondering what came next.

'Gunsmith, eh?'

Keith agreed.

'If I go through with firing salute over grave, like to load that damned Roman Candle for me? Eh?'

Keith said that he would do so, at the same time vowing to himself that, if he should happen to be present at the service, he would remain as far from the general as was possible. He and the general saw eye to eye on the subject of that particular weapon.

In the distance, a small field was occupied by several horses. 'Are those the horses mentioned in the will?' Enterkin asked.

'They would be,' the general said. 'Grass loved horses. Had to speak to him about it.' And the general glared at them, daring them to acknowledge that a joke had been made.

While Pru supervised the play of the general's dogs and grandchildren, the others went to find Colin Winter. He

42

occupied an old but lavishly modernised cottage (for Mr Grass had been a model landlord and employer), approached through a garden of mixed shrubs and vegatables. Mrs Winter sent them out to the back, where they found Winter at his rearing pens, feeding a couple of hundred pheasant poults. Keith, who had expected a larger scale of rearing on a rich man's estate, was impressed. It was his belief that a gamekeeper should not be a poultry-farmer.

Colin Winter was in his forties, brown-skinned and grey-haired. His face showed no expression. His voice held more than a trace of his Aberdeenshire origins. When he was excited, his eyes twinkled or flashed, his hair seemed to bristle and his tongue went right back to his ancestors. He seemed in no hurry to ingratiate himself with his visitors but, with minimal courtesy, offered them a seat on an old bench while himself remaining standing with the ease of a man who spends all of his life on foot.

Brutus lay down with his nose against the wire of a pen. This was a new scent to him, totally and utterly strange, yet it called to something deep inside him.

The general performed the introductions. Winter nodded dourly, but then a flicker of expression crossed his square face. 'Calder?' he said reflectively. Keith brightened – he was not averse to recognition by the shooting fraternity. 'The wildlife photographer?'

Keith deflated. 'My wife,' he said.

'Aye? Man, yon lassie can fairly catch the very soul of a creature,' Winter said. 'I've a calender of her work from the folk that supply the pheasant-feed. Just grand! You're a shooting man yoursel'?'

Mr Enterkin suppressed a smile. 'Mr Calder's a gunsmith as well as a shooting man. He's here to advise me about the shooting.'

43

'Indeed?' Winter looked at Keith and hesitated. 'Then maybe we'd better let him have a go at the pigeons while he's here.'

The general looked disgruntled at this theft of his thunder.

'I'd be very pleased,' Keith said.

Winter looked at Mr Enterkin. 'And yoursel'?' he asked.

Enterkin shook his head. 'I don't shoot,' he said. 'Not that I've anything against the practice. I have never understood why the Almighty should have endowed the same creatures with incontinent habits and the gift of flight.'

Keith hurried to change the subject before Mr Enterkin got onto the subject of the dawn chorus, of which he profoundly disapproved. 'Sad about Mr Grass's death,' he said.

'It was that,' said Winter.

'And surprising?'

That did it.

'Aye. M'hm. I just canna' understand it even yet. Spoke gey sharp to me once, just for stepping o'er a low fence. My gun was open, but wisna' empty. But then, he was gey canny, his-sel'.'

Keith remembered Sir Peter's words. 'People do set themselves a lower standard when they're alone.'

Winter bristled. 'Nae him. I found him, ye ken. Gey early in the day. I was just setting oot to go round my traps. He'd been lying there through the night. There'd been a frost for days so that the ground was showing nae marks; but you could almost see how he'd lost his balance and dropped the gun.'

'You think that's what happened?'

'I've aye had ma doots. He just wasna' the man to dae that, nae matter fit the police mak' oot.'

'Even if he was in a hurry?' Enterkin asked.

'Fit way would he be in ony brattle?'

'If he'd spotted a poacher?' Keith suggested.

Winter hesitated and then, surprisingly, half-smiled before shaking his head. 'He was hurried most o' his working life. But when he was here and awa' fae it a', it was his time to relax. He'd just tak' a gun and go for what he called a "footle-about". Whiles, he'd just come doon here for a wee crack.' Winter sighed. 'It was efter the end of the season, so he'd just be efter a rabbit or a pigeon. There was plenty of baith about, but his game-bag was empty. His heid was an awfu' mess. Ye ken they had a job to mak' out if it was himsel' or not. I did wonder, for a while, if it wasna' ane o' his jokes that went wrong. But no. I'll not believe that. Not wi' a corpus.'

Mr Enterkin broke an awkward silence. 'I have to see a Joe Merson in one of the cottages,' he said. 'Where would that be?'

Winter's face hardened. He jerked his head. 'About a quarter-mile down towards the loch. I dinna' ken why the master ever let him bide, the bugger of a poacher that he is. But Mr Grass seemed to like the old rogue. Anyway, he's not been seen here since February. Off to the mountains poaching stags, likely, he's done that afore and been nabbed at it.'

Keith and Mr Enterkin caught each other's eye. 'He's been gone since about the time Mr Grass died?' Keith said.

'Aye. Just about. He was here a few days after – I'm certain sure, because I'd been down to the station to sign my state-ment and I saw Joe Merson in the village. Then at gloamin', the same nicht, I heard shots from down by the loch. You'll ken how the sound can carry in a frost. I went out, but I saw naebody; and in the mornin' there'd been a touch of snow. Any marks were away. I've not seen him since, or heard him either; and I don't want to, except that I could be doing with a fresh bag of shot. He's the only man can pour good shot

45

around here, and it's cheaper than you can get in the shops. If he'd stick to that and a little ferreting and leave my pheasants alone, I could thole him.'

'That's a bit of a coincidence, isn't it?' Keith asked.

'Aye, it is. It made me think, but I've thocht and thocht, wondering whether the two of them hadna' gone off on some ploy together. I canna' believe it, though they were thick as thieves, those two. You'd hardly credit it, a millionaire and a scruffy old tink. But Joe used to help Mr Grass with some of his wee jokes at times. He loaded some funny cartridges, to put among the general's.'

'He did, did he?' General Springburn said ominously.

'Aye.' Clearly, any revenge that the general might care to exact would be all right with Winter.

This reminder of the "little coloured bubbles" had unsettled the general. He climbed stiffly to his feet. 'Leave you to it,' he suggested.

'You may well stay,' Enterkin said. 'You too, Keith. It's the future of the estate that I want to discuss.'

The general subsided with an audible creak. Winter's face froze again. Keith thought that the man was well named.

Enterkin paused to gather up his words. He half-turned on the bench so that all three men were within the radius of his attention. 'One of Mr Grass's regrets,' he said, 'was a rift that exists between shooting men and naturalists. He felt that a great opportunity for understanding and collaboration was being lost.'

'That's true enough,' the general said. 'Most responsible shooting men are naturalists at heart, but there's a new breed of birdwatcher comes out from the cities at weekends with a pair of binoculars and a book of birds.'

'Aye,' Winter said, 'and thinkin' that he'd be doing the pretty birdies a favour if he could ban the shooting altogether.'

Mr Enterkin raised his eyebrows. 'And he wouldn't?' he asked incautiously.

The other three gasped at this heresy.

'Of course not,' Keith said. 'The shooting man has more incentive for positive action than anybody else. He needs a rich wildlife scene.'

'He attends to the habitat,' Winter said, 'and feeds the woods when the feeding's scarce.'

'And keeps the predators in check,' said the general.

'*And* poachers,' Keith said. 'Try to understand. The ecology of this country descends from a thousand years of the inter-action between farming and hunting. Some species may have been hunted out, but very few. Far more have died out because their habitat changed. Others have been imported for their sporting potential, and survive because they suit the new conditions and because they are cosseted. That cosset-ting – the feeding, the preserving of cover – spins off into the rest of wildlife. A lot of responsible naturalists know that, but this new breed, they have a dreamy vision of going back to an idyllic balance of nature –'

'Wi' sabre-toothed tigers and hairy elephants,' Winter put in contemptuously.

'– but, in fact, if the economic pressure from shooting stopped, the habitat would suffer as the farmers started crop-ping the marginal corners of the land. Feeding would stop. So would the harvesting of surplus wildlife. A hell of a lot would starve to death in a bad winter. But they don't want to know about that.'

'The pheasant would virtually die out in a few years,' the general said.

'The partridge might last a bittie longer,' Winter said. 'But the crows'd begin to dominate the landscape, an' the song bird'd tak' a beating. D'ye ken, I've seen a magpie tak' eight

47

fledglings in a day, from other birds' nests, to feed its own. He took nothing the next day, because I shot the bugger. But who'd dae that if the land wasna' keepered?' He glared at Mr Enterkin.

'I only asked,' the solicitor said plaintively. 'There's no need to read me a lecture.'

'There's every need,' Keith said. 'Pigeon and rabbit would have to be poisoned, or subjected to germ-warfare. Do you think they'd like that?'

'All *right*,' Mr Enterkin said. 'You've put your viewpoint across. I'll decide in my own good time whether I accept it, without you raving at me like a bunch of fanatics.' He got out his notes and hid his face in them. 'Mr Grass's will provides for the future upkeep of the estate, which will be used as a training centre in ecology. It will be run by a trust on which all wildlife interests will be represented, the primary aim of the trust being projects of wildlife conservation, including research, anywhere in the country. Generous funds can be available, and special provision has been made for the services of scientific bodies.'

Mr Enterkin paused, and the others exchanged a dull glance. 'That's all gey fine,' Winter said gloomily. 'Grand for some. But it'll be the end of this estate as I've known it.'

'Perhaps,' Mr Enterkin said. 'I wouldn't know. The funds are to be made available in proportion to the revenue obtained for the shooting.'

There was another brief silence. Again it was Winter, whose thought-processes were surprisingly swift, who spoke first. 'Is anything said about the number of birds to be released?'

'Never to be more than five hundred in any one year.'

Keith gave a little whistle of appreciation. 'Clever!' he said.

Pleasure and relief were detectable on Winter's solid

features, but it was not in him to express them. 'I'll be needing more money,' he said.

Enterkin looked at him coldly. 'An increase in salary is specified, plus lecturer's fees. Your two sons can remain as your assistants if you so wish.'

Winter shook his head impatiently. 'I mean danger money,' he said. 'Unless we're sonsie enough to find a real good syndicate, it'll mean letting the shooting by the day. An undisciplined rabble o' Continentals and Yanks wi' repeating magnums. Och, I seen it a' before. By the time the birds are o'er their heids, they've wandered a'roads. An' it's suits of armour we'll need for the beaters.'

'You're right,' the general said. Winter's eyebrows shot up. The general began to glare.

'I think,' Enterkin said hastily, 'that we've covered enough ground for the moment. The details can await another occasion. We'd better be getting back to the inn.' He and Keith excused themselves and set off, leaving behind the mutter and grumble of guerilla warfare.

'We're not far from the house,' Keith said. 'Couldn't we just go round that way and take a preliminary look at the guns?'

'My feet tell me that I've walked enough for today.'

'It's doing you good.'

'When I want to be done good,' Mr Enterkin said, 'I'll ask. Not very loudly, but ask I will.' He loosened his collar and mopped his face. 'The staff aren't expecting us until tomorrow, so let's not throw them into a tizzy.'

'I'd have liked to make a start on the guns.'

'You've made a start on the estate, so be thankful. Do you really think,' Enterkin asked anxiously, 'that this trust's a good idea?'

'Yes, I do. I can just picture a bunch of slightly hostile wild-lifers in hot pursuit of the funds, running the estate for the shooting. They'll be heavily dependant on the raising of wild broods, so they'll soon find out that there's more to conservation than controlling the human predator. I don't see any of 'em killing over the heads of it, though. When can we pay a visit to the local fuzz?'

'If by that you mean the respected local constabulary, how about tomorrow afternoon after we've seen the household?'

'And the guns,' Keith said. 'All right.'

'Good. And now, hopefully for the last time today, let's put our best foot forward. A great hunger is coming over me. What's more, the inn has a wine list obviously tailored for Mr Grass's more demanding guests, and the prices are several years out of date. You couldn't get such bargains in a supermarket.'

SIX

As Mr Enterkin had suggested, the inn's cellar presented excellent value for money. They dined well on roast duckling. Later, they retired to the private bar, for discussion and further sustenance.

From behind the bar, the cuddlesome barmaid studied them unobtrusively. For most of his life the darkly handsome Keith had had and enjoyed, without ever being conscious of it, a sexual magnetism for women. He would have been piqued to know that the barmaid had dismissed him after a glance as being good-looking in a rather obvious way, probably a lady-killer and of no real interest. Mr Enterkin, she thought, was something else again. He dressed well, which she liked. He was older, but she herself was no longer a girl and she had come to prefer the mature male. His noticeable chubbiness made her feel alluringly slim by comparison. She liked a man who enjoyed good cooking, and from what she had glimpsed in the dining room no man ever enjoyed it more. His voice was educated, and his grandiloquent turn of phrase pleased and impressed her. He was a gentleman.

Keith and Mr Enterkin, over their brandies, had drifted from the subject of estate management into more specialised topics. Mr Enterkin was trying hard to understand.

'Take grouse and partridge,' Keith said. 'They're very territorial birds. They respond to heavy shooting – you get a larger and more vigorous population the following season. The reason is that when they're unshot the older males take over more and more territory and the younger and more vigorous birds don't get a chance to breed. They're like people, really. The older cocks are probably infertile anyway.' He looked at his watch. 'Here, I'd better phone Molly.'

There was a public phone in the hall. Keith got through to Molly and reassured her that he was safe and adequately nourished. 'Has Jack Waterhouse been yet?' he asked.

'He phoned,' Molly said. 'I think he's going to pay your price for the Baker rifle. He's coming over tomorrow.'

'Right.' Keith thought for a moment. 'Never mind what I said. Don't be too rude to him. I think, from what I hear, I'm going to need his help.'

Mr Enterkin had taken Keith's remark personally, which had not been Keith's intention. 'I'm not infertile,' he told the empty room. He bounced up and rapped on the bar. The barmaid came through the back-bar door from the other room.

'Ask him yourself,' she said over her shoulder. She supplied Mr Enterkin with another brandy-and-soda and took his money. 'You're the solicitor,' she said.

Mr Enterkin said that he was.

'The lads through there are wondering if there's anything in the will for any of them.'

He shook his head. 'Apart from some minor tenancy matters, anybody mentioned in the will has had a letter by now. Except for one person that we didn't have an address for. A lady.'

There was a concerted groan from the other room. She shut the door. 'My name's Laing,' she said. 'Mrs Helen Laing. They call me Penny, of course.'

'I'm afraid there's nothing for you. Should there have

52

been?' He asked the question without any ulterior thoughts except to continue a conversation with a pretty woman and to listen to an accent which still delighted him. He was surprised and disconcerted to see her blush.

'He didn't owe me anything,' she said seriously. 'Not for want of asking, but with him that didn't mean anything. He tried it on with every woman for miles around.'

'Not always unsuccessfully?'

She paused before speaking. Enterkin guessed that her habit was to attend silently behind the bar, taking in the gossip but never joining in. 'You can't believe talk,' she said at last. 'Not around here, there's too much of it. But on looks alone, there must be three of his bastards in this village. There!'

Mr Enterkin knew from the will that there were five, but could hardly say so. 'And he had the reputation of being a careful man with a gun,' he said.

Penny laughed aloud, so that her figure jiggled deliciously. 'He mayn't have been too careful with some of the shots he fired,' she said.

'The local ladies would seem to have remained undeterred.'

Penny went back to polishing glasses. It was her substitute for knitting. 'No. But he was very generous. If you see a fur coat in the village, or a string of pearls, or a sports car . . . And the good Lord alone knows how many gifts may be hidden away and not shown in the street at all. And then the unmarried ones may have been hoping, and the married ones had little enough to lose. And, you know,' she said thoughtfully, 'he had a lot of charm. When he told a girl that she was beautiful, he could almost make her believe that he meant it.'

Most of Penny's argument in mitigation of female frailty

passed Mr Enterkin by, but her last remark caught his attention. Between the influences of food and wine (not to mention spirits), a charming woman and his own verbosity, he was in a state close to euphoria. In common with the general and the late Mr Grass, he had his own personal imp of mischief which was usually in safe confinement somewhere between his frontal lobes. Now he felt his control slipping.

To his own astonishment he picked up Penny's hand and heard his own voice speaking. 'If I were paying court to you,' he said softly, 'I wouldn't waste words telling you what your own mirror must tell you every morning, or that you have the kind of figure that men have given up empires for...' she was trying to pull her hand away, but not very hard, '... or that you have eyes,' he added, noticing for the first time that she did indeed have eyes, and very blue and bright they were.

Keith's head came round the door — rather to Mr Enterkin's relief, for he had found himself quite unable to think of anything to say about Penny's eyes which had not already been said, and better, by the poets.

'Sorry to drink and run,' Keith said; 'but I think I'll walk the dog, and then I'm for my bed.'

'That's all right,' said Mr Enterkin. 'See you in the morning.'

'Good night, then.'

'Good night.'

Penny had managed to keep busy without quite removing her hand from reach. Mr Enterkin gathered that the moment had not, after all, passed. 'What were we talking about?' she asked innocently.

'Nothing.'

'Nothing?'

54

'Surely,' Mr Enterkin said, 'telling you what I wouldn't say is talking about nothing.'

'What – what would you say, then?'

He recaptured her hand. 'Nor could I promise you jewels or sports cars.'

Her hand lost a little of its warmth. 'What, then?'

He spoke very softly, almost into her ear. Just what he promised must remain their secret. He whispered on and on, and this time there were no interruptions. Penny breathed more quickly and her knees felt rubbery.

Very early in the morning, Penny Laing stretched luxuriously. She slipped out of bed and started to dress, a process which Mr Enterkin watched with fresh pleasure. His comfortable arrangement, recently terminated, had been with an astringent divorcee of enormous libido but many inhibitions, and he had forgotten the thrill of burrowing in warm satin to find the delights beneath, and the converse but equally exquisite pleasure of watching a lady dress.

'You may be good,' Penny said teasingly, 'but you're not as good as you said you were.'

He chuckled. 'So never trust a lawyer.'

'I don't. Anyway, my dear, you're better than Mr Grass was – from what I've heard. Girls talk, you know.'

'I know they do. They talk to lawyers, mostly.'

'And I thought that lawyers never did anything dangerous.'

'Our motto is, if you do something dangerous do it safely.'

She paused in that most feminine gesture, twisting to fasten a back suspender. Penny Laing had never taken to tights. 'I hope so,' she said. 'There's enough of those in the village already. Well, at least you're a proper gent in a bed. Mr Grass wasn't always, or so I'm told.'

55

'He still seemed to have his share of successes.'

'He wasn't above applying a little pressure. Money pressure. So I'm told.'

'For all his methods,' Mr Enterkin said, 'it seems that I got something that he didn't. Or so I'm told.'

She smoothed down her dress and came and sat beside him on the bed. 'You can believe this or not,' she said, 'just as you like, but you're the first since my husband died. I don't know what came over me tonight, really I don't.'

'I believe you. And I'm looking forward to our dinner.'

'You don't have to come,' she said anxiously. 'Not if you don't really want to.'

'I want to,' he said.

SEVEN

Keith was not surprised when Mr Enterkin slept late the next morning, for the solicitor had strong views about early rising. He was against it.

Brutus, on the other hand, had been up and about for hours and greeted Keith with enthusiasm. *Eat up. Master'll sleep for ages. Let's go somewhere.* Keith hurried his breakfast, and as they strolled round to the general's house he sifted and sorted the facts and gossip surrounding the death of Raymond Grass. Just as a melody of haunting beauty might be flawed by two or three false notes, so the pattern surrounding the death was perfect but for the character of the man and the quality of his gun. Those discrepancies might not impress the police, but they chafed Keith's mind like blisters on a heel.

The general seemed to be waiting, but he waved aside Keith's apologies for tardiness. 'Didn't expect you to be up and about early this morning,' the general boomed, and he winked slyly. Keith wondered what he meant but was not sufficiently interested to ask.

The gun was produced and Keith tried it to his shoulder while the general took out a supply of cartridges. The gun was clean and well-kept and the fit seemed good. Another matter was bothering Keith. 'You know Joe Merson, General?' he asked. 'What did he look like?'

The general pondered. 'Scarecrow.'

'Physical attributes?' Keith found the general's clipped speech infectious.

'Ah.' The general pondered again. 'Medium height. Thickset. Gingery. Nose like Concorde. Otherwise unremarkable.'

'Did he resemble Raymond Grass at all?'

'Similar height and colour. Faces different.'

'Did you see Joe Merson around at all after Mr Grass died?'

The general looked at Keith in mild surprise. 'Not that I remember. You don't think —?'

'I was just wondering. Nobody else suggested such a thing?'

'Not that I heard.'

Keith knew that the speed and accuracy of a village grape-vine was conditioned by social undercurrents that the newcomer might take months to assess. 'Is this a gossipy place?' he asked.

The general looked at him curiously. 'You'll find out,' he said. 'Well, can't have you walking about like that. Look as if you were going to rob a bank. Here.' He produced a gun-slip and an elderly game-bag.

Keith made suitably grateful noises.

'About due to go out myself,' the general said wistfully. 'Exercise dogs. Might have a little sport together?' He brandished another gun. Keith ducked aside.

Keith felt no inclination to go shooting with anyone as casual with guns as the general, but he had no wish to hurt the feelings of an old man. He excused himself on the grounds that his objective was the training of Brutus, which would not be possible in the presence of other dogs.

'Quite right,' said the general reluctantly. 'Might have an outing or two later, if I can persuade Pru to walk my beasts?'

'Possibly.' Keith scoured his mind for a way out. 'I doubt we'd get much if you're in your white coat; except maybe shooting over ferrets.'

The general closed his eyes for a second. 'I have permission to shoot another farm, off the estate,' he said.

'I'm here to advise about the Whinkirk House Estate. I shouldn't go stravaiging.'

'Well,' said the general as if the idea had only just struck him, 'perhaps you could put in a word with Enterkin, eh? Liberal interpretation of the rules?'

'I'll see what I can do,' Keith said.

The general brightened slightly. But his interpretation of Keith's words may not have tallied closely with their intent.

Back at the inn, Keith found Mr Enterkin up at last and working his way through a substantial breakfast. The solicitor, who was usually at his worst at what he regarded as the very crack of dawn, surprised Keith by being in an unwontedly sunny and benevolent mood. He was, however, stern in his refusal to walk to Whinkirk House. 'I have telephoned,' he said. 'The Rolls will call for me shortly.'

'Why drive the long way round? It's a grand day again, and only a mile or so to walk.'

'A mile or so as the crow flies,' Enterkin said, 'but three at least if you follow the field boundaries. I've no great fancy to go striding about the farms. You walk, my dear chap, and I'll see you there about eleven. Take Brutus with you if you like,' he added generously.

'You want to come with me, Brutus?' Keith asked.

Brutus hesitated for less than a second. His master might be good for titbits, but instinct told him that Keith was going in the direction of his own true destiny.

They followed the route of the day before. As soon as the houses had tailed away and the farmland opened up, Keith loaded the general's gun. He fell again into a walking reverie. Of course, it was quite possible for a careful man to slip into carelessness just once, and to die for it. Raymond

59

Grass might have had cause to hurry. If he had seen a poacher, perhaps. Or hit a rabbit that was still struggling towards a hole — the ethic of the sport would oblige him to hurry and despatch it mercifully. It might depend on whether he had had a dog with him.

They were following the flank of the first strip of wood-land when a wood-pigeon came clattering out overhead. Keith's reactions took over before he could bring his mind back from its wanderings. He mounted and swung, pulled the trigger as his barrels passed the bird, and the pigeon in mid-air turned into a bundle of meat and feathers. It landed thirty yards away.

True to his training, Brutus sat firm; but the shot had no more meaning than that. The order to "Fetch" puzzled him. No familiar object had been thrown, no dummy had sailed from the gun. He quested obediently over the ground, but there was nothing of interest. Only a piece of feathered meat, too fresh to eat. He came back and presented himself for reassurance.

Keith sighed, and they walked together to the dead bird which lay at the foot of a thick hedge. Brutus nosed it and then sat down for a scratch. Keith picked the bird, noticing as he did so that there was a snare set in the hedge. He was tempted to throw the pigeon for Brutus, but the loose-feathered bird would be a dangerous introduction to real game; in getting a firm grip, the young dog could become hard in the mouth. He stowed the bird in the net of the general's bag and walked on, discouraged.

There was really no reason why another man of similar build shouldn't decide to absent himself after the death of his patron.

Winter was working in his front garden, but seemed not displeased to straighten his back. He nodded at the game-bag. 'You've started then. How did the wee dog do?'

'As a gun-dog he'd make a fine pair of book-ends if I had another one,' Keith said. 'He wouldn't look at it. I don't think he's ever met the real thing. I was wondering about trying him on a cold rabbit. Or would your wife be able to give me an old stocking, or a foot off a pair of tights?'

'Aye. That often helps.'

Brutus knew that he was glad to be back, without understanding why. This was where it all happened, whatever it was. He disappeared around the corner, ignoring Winter's half-bred spaniel, and lay down with his nose against the wire of the pen.

Winter put his head in at the cottage door and then took a seat beside Keith, on a low wall warmed by the sun. He produced some papers from his hip pocket. 'Just to be proper, I got each farmer to write you out a note.'

'Thanks.' Keith took the letters. 'How did you manage it? Getting a farmer to write something down's usually like trying to get a cat to take a bath.'

Winter smiled faintly. 'I've no doubt they'll be wanting something in return, seeing as Mr Enterkin will be looking to you about the running of the estate. Mr Yates at North Farm said to tell you he'd be glad of a word shortly.'

Mrs Winter brought out the desired tube of nylon, and with it a tray of tea, in large mugs, and biscuits. She smiled cosily without saying a word and went back indoors. The men drank their tea in companionable silence.

'You've a lot of pheasant broods in the wild,' Keith said at last.

'That's what it's all about.'

'Partridges, too.'

'Aye.'

'You believe in the Euston system?'

Winter thawed at last. 'Tried it,' he said. 'But there's more work lifting eggs and incubating them and putting them back than there is in controlling the predators and keeping them on the move for a few weeks. If the cover's just right for rearing a brood, they'll rear in the wild.'

Keith let him talk on. It was a pleasure to hear an expert enthusiast on his own subject. Winter knew wildlife as easily as Keith himself could read a proof-mark.

When the keeper fell silent, Keith said, 'Are you sure that you saw Joe Merson after Mr Grass was shot?'

'Just a shape in the distance.'

Keith hesitated. 'Could it have been Mr Grass?' he asked suddenly.

Winter seemed relieved that the question had been asked. 'I did think about that,' he said. 'Even when I saw the body, with the face a' smashed, I thought to mysel' that I couldn't have told it from Merson's but for the claes. But no. The mannie I saw took wee steps like Joe Merson. Joe aye just shuffled along. Mr Grass took great strides.'

'But you don't know of anybody seeing Joe Merson for sure?'

'No, I don't. But why would I?' Winter asked reasonably. 'He wasn't such a rarity that they'd talk about him as if they'd seen a marsh sandpiper.'

'I suppose not. Did you hear a shot, or shots, the night Mr Grass was killed?'

'No. But I wouldn't, indoors. Those walls are thick.'

'But a few nights later you heard shots down by the lake?'

'I was out fetching clugs from the pile.' Winter nodded at the log-pile by the cottage's gable.

'Ah.' Keith thought that he had stretched Winter's patience as far as was safe for the moment.

While they spoke, Keith had dropped the pigeon into the

nylon foot and tied the end. He showed it to Brutus, who had returned from his meditations by the pheasant-pen, and then threw the bundle for him to retrieve. With the pigeon enclosed and now cold, Brutus performed perfectly.

'That'll likely do it,' Winter said. 'But you'd better keep the bittie stocking, just in case.'

'Would you like the pigeon?' Keith asked.

'Aye, I'll take it gladly. Mary makes a grand pie.' Winter paused. There was a visible struggle between his natural reserve and his desire to make overtures to Keith, in whom he had found some kinship of the spirit. 'You'll be welcome to join us any evening. You'll have another engagement the nicht, though.'

'Will I? I suppose so,' Keith said vaguely. He could hardly have guessed that the butcher, whose van had called earlier in the morning, had remarked that Penny Laing had bought two steaks instead of her usual chop. 'One last thing,' he said. 'I noticed a wire snare on the way along. Yours?'

Winter shook his head emphatically. 'My sons do the trapping, but we only allow Fenn traps. Unless . . . but they'd no' dare. It's a' right, Mr Calder,' he added. 'I ken who it'll be. Just you leave him to me.'

'You're being poached?'

'Aye. I'll tell my boys to keep an eye out. And you'd best keep an eye open for them, and make yoursel' known if you meet them, or they're likely to run you off as a poacher. You canna' mistake them, twa muckle loons,' Winter raised his hand to indicate a height of nearly eight feet, 'wi' backsides on them like a pair of elephants.'

Following Winter's directions, Keith and Brutus set off for Whinkirk House by a path that threaded the fields from wood to wood. Keith was walking with what Winter would have called "great strides". He tried a shuffling gait. It was easy to disguise his walk. Then he felt silly and looked round to be sure that nobody had seen him.

Soon their path began to climb an embankment topped by a fence. This, according to Winter, was where Mr Grass had died, but there was no sign of the tragedy. Ever-changing nature tolerates no memorials.

The embankment was heavily covered with brambles and all the growth that takes place in the bramble's protection. It was an ideal place for wildlife, and indeed Keith could hear the rustling and scratching of many birds. Rabbits, too, had made paths through the grass and nettles. Perhaps there had once been the corpse of a rabbit which had crept in to die, Keith thought, a rabbit which had been the cause of Mr Grass's haste and carelessness. But, if so, the sexton beetles would have disposed of it long since, if a fox had not found it first. Brutus penetrated a few yards along a rabbit run, and a great cock pheasant rocketed up with a whirr and an indignant squawk. Brutus retired against Keith's leg.

Brutus had something in his mouth. Just to be safe, Keith made him give it up. It was a piece of greaseproof paper, old and weathered, that smelled both sweet and vinous. Some time ago, an old poacher's trick had been used here. A pheasant, shrouded and panicking, might well have been enough to make Mr Grass forget his cautious habits.

Keith unloaded carefully and climbed the fence.

EIGHT

Whinkirk House, when they reached it, turned out to be a small eighteenth century mansion set on a slight rise and seeming to grow out of a foundation of flowers, because the terraces that ringed it were edged with a cataract of rock-plants. The house, a mixture of white roughcast and the red local stone, stood up bravely in the sunlight. The surrounding trees with their accompanying underbrush, so typical of a shooting estate, were kept at bay by broad lawns.

They were received at the door by a small, elderly man who managed to combine great dignity with an air of bustle and an eye that held a twinkle of mischief. He relieved Keith of the gun and bag as if it were quite normal for a guest to arrive bearing arms, which in that house was probably the case. Dogs, he said, were no problem; but Mr Grass's springer spaniel bitch, Champion Wortleberry of Whinkirk, was at present in season and confined to kennels.

'We have of course been expecting you, sir,' he added. 'Mr Enterkin is here. He invited the staff to join you both for coffee as soon as you arrived.'

As he was led through the house, Keith did a little mental arithmetic. Champion Wortleberry of Whinkirk would have been out of season when Mr Grass died unless her metabolic clock were quite abnormally rapid.

The solicitor was waiting in what had been Mr Grass's study, a large room with French windows opening onto a sunny terrace.

Brutus lay down under the desk, out of the way of

trampling feet. His acute instincts, deriving mainly from inherited understanding of scents detected by a nose a thousand times as sensitive as a man's, fed him messages about people and animals, past and present. Above all, he was sure that this had been a happy place, but now it was sad and filled with uncertainty. One person in it was frightened.

Keith, for his part, was looking around. Instead of pictures Mr Grass's study was hung with examples from his collection of firearms. Almost immediately, Keith's eye lit on the Roman Candle. He stood in front of it and Enterkin heaved himself up and came to stand beside Keith. 'That's it, is it?' he asked.

'That's it.'

'What's so special about it? It's just a four-barrelled pistol.'

Keith went to take it down, but the gun was securely attached to the wall. 'It's what the general called it, a contraption, an early attempt to get extra fire-power. One of the barrels –' he checked the position of the flashpan '– the top one, fires normally. Two, or all three, of the others contain several loads superimposed, and an interconnecting series of touch-holes fires each load in turn. You hope. If it works like that, you've got a small machine-gun. If it doesn't, you've got a bomb.'

'Would you fire it?' Enterkin asked anxiously.

'Yes. But I'd tie it to a tree and use a long string. I think I'd better test-fire it that way before the general gets his hands on it. And if I'm at the service, I'll be at the other end of the throng. Would it be acceptable if I loaded it with blank charges?'

The solicitor was tempted. But if Keith loaded the piece it should be safe enough. 'The will is specific,' he said reluctantly. 'It says "Loaded with ball".'

'That's that, then.'

A jingling trolley of coffee cups interrupted them.

The dignified servitor introduced himself a Roach, butler and valet to Mr Grass. His wife, as elderly as himself and on the verge of frailty, was both cook and housekeeper. There was one maid, a blue-eyed blonde by the name of Bessie, who doubled as assistant cook. Bert Hayes, the chauffeur-gardener who had driven them from Newton Lauder, was a gnarled little man of uncertain age.

The other person present, and the only one with but a single job, was Miss Alice Wyper. She had been Mr Grass's personal secretary. She was a tall brunette. Nature had been liberal to her with nose and bosom and, Keith decided, had not been ungenerous in the matter of backsides either. She looked thirty, but was probably five years older. She was elegantly but inexpensively dressed.

By the time that courtesies had been exchanged, coffee dispensed and he had them seated around him in an expectant semi-circle – rather like performing seals, Enterkin thought, waiting for their fish – the ice had been broken and there was a general but distrait conversation. The relationship between them seemed to be more like that of a family than the stiff hierarchy that usually develops in the service of large houses.

When Enterkin cleared his throat there was immediate silence. 'We seem to be a very small party for this size of house,' he said.

'Mr Grass was here on in his own for much of the time,' Miss Wyper said, 'when he was here at all.'

'He did not like to have more staff around him than were necessary for his own needs,' said Roach.

'There's daily help comes in as needed,' Bessie explained.

'And caterers for special occasions,' said Mrs Roach. 'Under my direction,' she added firmly.

67

That much being explained, Mr Enterkin went on to expound the future of the house and the estate, and to stress that they could all consider themselves secure in their jobs. 'Mr and Mrs Roach will be expecting to retire shortly and this has been provided for, although I am hoping – I'm sure we all hope – that they will remain at least for some months until new arrangements have been both made and proven.' There was an assenting murmur, and the Roaches bowed in dignified unison. 'Bessie and Mr Hayes have already received letters notifying them of personal bequests, but I shall be pleased to see them individually if they so wish. I shall certainly want to speak to Mr and Mrs Roach shortly about the pension arrangements. And I think that it would be better if I saw Miss Wyper personally, to explain the conditions attaching to her legacy.'

The elegant Miss Wyper chose this moment to turn white and spill her coffee into her lap, and the discussion was disrupted for some minutes while damp cloths were fetched and applied.

When he had their full attention again, Mr Enterkin made a short speech. It seemed to be expected of him, he told himself. He thanked them for their loyalty in the past on behalf of the late Mr Grass, but asked them to accept the fact of his passing and to turn their minds and their loyalties to the future. Finding his audience with him, he ventured a small joke which was well received and then dismissed the company. 'Perhaps,' he added, 'Mr and Mrs Roach would like to remain and discuss the pension arrangements?'

Roach smiled deprecatingly. 'Mrs Roach deals with all matters of a financial nature,' he said. 'I'll be getting about my business.'

Keith decided that the Roaches' pension could hardly fall within his province. 'Perhaps Mr Roach would show me the house,' he suggested.

'A good arrangement,' said Enterkin. 'Then we could see Miss Wyper together.'

Miss Wyper blanched again.

The tour of the house took some time. Keith, who was not a total stranger to luxury, was impressed by the quality and condition of every item that he saw, right down to the kitchen utensils. Mr Grass had not hesitated to spend his money, provided that there was a proper return in human comfort or happiness. He had not been such a saint as to count anyone else's happiness higher than his own, but Keith noticed that the humblest staff bedroom would not have been out of place in a good hotel. He counted six excellent bathrooms, and the central heating ran throughout the house. In the outbuildings, he was shown the garage with Hayes' quarters above and the cars gleaming inside.

He met the ailing spaniel, leaving Brutus sitting indignantly in the yard. He thought that the springer bitch looked narrow in the head for showing. 'You called her a champion,' he said. 'Was that in field trials?'

Roach drew himself up an extra inch. 'Certainly, sir. Mr Grass was not a devotee of the show-bench. Ruination of a good working breed, he called it.'

'So do I. But I don't remember seeing her. Who worked her in trials? Winter?'

'Mr Grass always worked her himself.'

Roach led the way back into the yard. Brutus welcomed them with an ecstasy partly due to the scent of the confined lady.

'Was she out with Mr Grass, the night he died?' Keith asked.

'No, sir.' Roach hesitated. He looked at Keith out of the corner of his eye, and must have decided that he was not too sensitive to be exposed to the facts of life. 'When Mr Grass was going visiting, some of his friends did not like a dog in the house. Of course, Wortles would lie at a front door and never move, but Mr Grass didn't like to leave her on a doorstep.'

'And was he going visiting that night?'

'Mr Grass did not confide in us. But he said that nobody was to wait up, and that he would not want to be called in the morning.'

So Mr Grass had been on the way to, or from, a lady, Keith decided, drawing on his own experience.

'Would you happen to know which of Mr Grass's friends disliked having a dog in the house?'

'I wouldn't know about that at all,' Roach said. He pondered for a moment, and there was a mischievous gleam in his eye. 'The information should not be difficult to obtain. Mr Grass's will should give a clear indication of his circle of acquaintances. And you do have a dog.'

Keith looked at him sharply. 'Roach, you're pulling my leg.'

'Just a little bit, sir.' Roach wheezed with ancient laughter and led the way back into the house.

Keith supposed that the process of natural selection would result in the house of an amorous bachelor being staffed by persons with a certain breadth of mind.

'Did he have only the one dog?' he asked.

'He was thinking of starting another in training. Mr Grass's younger dog was shot during the winter. Sheep-chasing. Very unfortunate. It was after that incident that Mr Grass stopped leaving Wortles outside.'

'You're trying to pull my leg again, aren't you?' Keith asked. 'No lady would let the male Lothario leave his dog on her doorstep at night. It'd be as bad as a bicycle.'

Roach twinkled again. 'Were we talking about ladies, sir? I didn't realise. I thought we were talking about dogs.' He paused outside the study door. 'But doorsteps hereabouts can be a long way from the road. We've plenty of room here, as you can see. It would be no trouble to have you stay here.'

The sudden change of subject disconcerted Keith or he might have seen its implications. 'That's very kind of you,' he said. 'But I'm very comfortable at the inn.'

'I never doubted it. But young ladies have never presented any problem in this house. And it is perhaps more discreet than the inn.'

'I'll go along with what Mr Enterkin wants,' Keith said. It seemed that feudalism was far from dead at Whinkirk House. He wondered if he would be expected to take seigneural rights of Bessie, as he supposed Mr Grass had done.

Miss Wyper received them in a large office, severely but very well equipped and furnished. Brutus sniffed the air and decided, *this is the frightened one.*

Keith had a sharp ear for accents, and Miss Wyper's was of good class, possibly Cheltenham followed by Girton − if genuine, he thought. She bore a general resemblance to a rather jolly hockey mistress, but at the moment a rather subdued games mistress watching the match of the year being thrown away. She was too nervous to sit down, so the two men had to stand.

In a vain attempt to put her at ease, Enterkin complimented her on the orderliness of the office and of Mr Grass's papers generally, and expressed a hope that she would stay to keep order for many years to come.

'I hope so too,' she said quickly, almost gabbling. 'I hope so very much. I know about the trust, of course, I typed all Mr Grass's notes. I can't sympathise with the objectives, can't approve the spilling of blood, but as long as I'm not expected to handle dead things −' she gave a ladylike shiver '− I'll be

71

happy to look after the office. I'm hoping to get married quite soon, but my fiance works on a whaling factory-ship so that I'll be free most of the time and the money will come in useful. Now,' she slowed down and took a deep breath, 'Mr Enterkin, you seemed to be implying that my legacy wasn't quite as straightforward as the rest. I hope I didn't quite understand you?'

'There is a condition attached to it,' said Enterkin.

Miss Wyper stole a frightened glance at Keith, whose presence seemed to perturb her. 'But there *can't* be. I typed all his codicils. Mr Grass wrote them all out in longhand. Sometimes his writing was all over the place because he couldn't help laughing. I had to smile myself, sometimes. But I typed them all up in proper form, and we got them witnessed and sent to you, and once a year they were embodied in a new will. He left me two thousand pounds without any conditions at all.'

'This reached me last autumn, as a codicil. It was in holograph form, and I'm afraid the writing was all over the place. But it was properly signed and, being holograph, did not need to be witnessed.'

She twisted her hands together, almost wringing them. 'But we *need* the money, to get married,' she said, as if that argument would surely be conclusive. 'We must have a home. And we've hardly a bean between us.'

'The new codicil,' Enterkin said quickly, 'allows you ten thousand pounds, or alternatively the cottage known as Elmlea.'

Her mouth fell open. Her teeth, Keith noticed, had also been provided by the Almighty in lavish mood. 'Oh,' she said.

'There is, as I said, a condition.'

'What is the condition?' Although her voice was strained the accent never slipped, which confirmed Keith in his opinion that it was genuine.

72

'The condition. Yes.' Enterkin hesitated and took refuge in his notes. 'You will appreciate that this was Mr Grass's own idea. The condition is that you attend the funeral – or in this case I should say the memorial service –'

'Oh, please hurry up!'

'–dressed,' Mr Enterkin said bravely, 'only in the fur of rabbits which you yourself have shot and skinned.'

Miss Wyper's reaction to this revelation was all that Mr Enterkin had feared, outdoing those of all the other legatees together. She uttered a faint squawk, turned slowly green and then rolled up her eyes and fainted. Roach, entering with her lunch on a tray, found Keith Calder trying to uphold both Miss Wyper and her personal modesty, and not succeeding very well with either.

Brutus, to his disgust (for he was in danger of becoming spoiled) was fed on the same nourishing kennel-meal as was provided for the incarcerated champion, but Keith and Mr Enterkin lunched in some style in Mr Grass's splendid dining room, all mirrors and polished wood. Keith never noticed that he was given the larger portions and the choicest morsels and Mr Enterkin, although indignant, was too well-mannered to protest but comforted himself with wine. Contrary to his prediction, an excellent claret appeared at the table.

'I need a few minutes more with the papers,' Enterkin said over the coffee cups. 'You go and see to Miss Wyper. Then we'll go and visit the police.'

'Oh no,' Keith said. 'You don't pass the buck to me. It's you she'll want to see.'

'I'm not having her fainting all down my chest. And she knows about the will now. You,' Mr Enterkin pointed out, 'are the one who can help her to comply with its terms.'

'I don't think she approves of me,' Keith said.

'Who does? I ask the question,' Mr Enterkin explained, 'not unkindly but out of a genuine desire for knowledge.'

Keith thought for several seconds. Of the first few people to come to mind, each had recently complained about some aspect of his conduct. 'Brutus does,' he said at last.

'Not a wholly disinterested approbation, but it will serve. There is something slightly doggy − note that I do not say "canine", nor yet "doggish" − about the lady's unstinting loyalty and conflicting impulses. If you can get through to my disloyal hound, you can surely bring Miss Wyper to heel.' Mr Enterkin was tempted to add flattery by alluding to Keith's reputedly winning ways with the human female, but just at the moment he himself was feeling a certain self-satisfaction in that area, and was unwilling to share credit even where credit was due.

Returning reluctantly upstairs, Keith found Miss Wyper recovered and picking at the offerings on her tray but now inclined to tears for which her features, and her usually hearty manner, were badly suited. She pushed the tray aside and dabbed at her eyes with an inadequate handkerchief. Out of unthinking courtesy Keith offered her his own, almost pristine, handkerchief. She took it and blew her nose violently. A feather from the morning's pigeon was left clinging below her damp nostril.

'How could he do such a thing?' she asked in a shuddering voice. 'After my years of service?'

'It's a generous legacy,' Keith said feebly. 'I'd jump at it.'

'But that condition!'

'It's nothing really very −'

She seemed not to hear him. 'He knew what it would mean to us. I'd told him about our wedding plans. And then to have me type out the bequest . . . So when Mr Grass died and I knew that I had the money coming I cabled Bill and he cabled back, and I've made an offer for a house in the village.'

Keith tried again. 'But you still have the money coming. More, in fact.'

But she broke down again, sobbing into his handkerchief so that he only caught her words in dissociated fragments. 'He knew how I deplore . . . shedding blood . . . God's creatures . . . little furry . . . nobody any harm.' She blew her nose again, transferring the feather to her chin, and started again. 'What you must think of me! But really, it's *too* much. He knew just how I felt. I never let it interfere with my job. If he wanted me to, I could get the best price for pheasant feed, organise the whole of a shooting weekend or market a thousand poor little corpses. But I never left him in any doubt about my feelings. I *hated* that side of it. I can't approve of killing things, and I could never bring myself to touch anything . . . *dead.*'

Keith breathed a secret sigh. He was being confronted by an unusually clearcut example of the combination of squeamishness and double standards which was familiar to him. With a certain type of city-dweller, he had found attitudes entrenched and argument a waste of breath; but in these surroundings and aided by Miss Wyper's motivation a few words might be worth a try.

'Are you a vegetarian?' he asked.

'No. But I don't see —'

'I think you do. Can you cook?'

'Certainly. Bill says that I'm an excellent cook.' She lifted her chin, feather and all.

'If I asked you to cook an oven-ready bird for me, could you do it?'

'Of course. Don't be silly.'

'If I asked you to buy a bird from a poulterer and pluck it and cook it, could you?'

This time she hesitated, but said that she thought that she could.

'Imagine that you're married to your Bill. He says that he'd just fancy a rabbit pie. The butcher has rabbits hanging in his window. Could you buy one, skin and clean it, and make him his pie?'

'I suppose so.'

'Then it's only a matter of mastering a few simple knacks and overcoming some personal scruples which can't be very deep-rooted.'

She looked hopeful and then sagged again. 'I couldn't do it.'

He nearly took hold of her and gave her a good shaking. 'Think what some of the others have to do,' he said. 'If you typed out the conditions . . .'

She managed a watery smile. 'Some of them don't seem to be minding very much. Old Mrs Mallison, for instance. She's at least old enough to be my mother if not my grandmother, but she says that after four husbands and . . . and I think she's exaggerating about her . . . her lovers,' Miss Wyper said firmly, 'she says that there can't be many mature men in the area who haven't seen it all before. Well, that's what she *says*.'

Keith suppressed a shudder. Mrs Mallison had made an appearance at the inn the previous evening. 'She may be putting a brave face on it,' he suggested. 'Whatever you feel, don't you think that your Bill might expect you to have a go?'

'I couldn't. I think it's wicked!'

'Rabbits have to be controlled. Working here, you must have seen how much damage they can do. If you were a rabbit, would you rather be controlled by being snared, or gassed, or subjected to myxomatosis, or chased out of your burrow by a ferret? Wouldn't you rather be shot?'

'But it's a sport!'

Keith gritted his teeth and decided on one last try. If this failed, she could throw her legacy down the drain and good luck to her when Bill found out. 'It wouldn't be a sport if you didn't enjoy it. There's an old story about a couple being married on a Saturday. The bridegroom explained to the minister that they wouldn't be reaching their honeymoon hotel until after midnight. Would they be forgiven, he asked, if they consummated their marriage on the Lord's Day? The minister thought it over and said, "It'll be all right *as long as you don't enjoy it*!" '

Miss Wyper looked shocked, but as she thought it over the irreverend logic of it seemed to impress her. He could see the hockey mistress resuming command of her again. 'Would you help me?' she asked.

'I think Mr Winter might be more suitable.'

'Oh no,' she said. 'I couldn't go to him. Not after some of the things I said to him.'

'I don't suppose he minded.'

'I said that he had blood on his hands.'

'Well, he probably did have.'

'He's so unsympathetic. He'd say things.'

'What about one of the farmers, then?'

She shook her head.

Keith was usually well paid for coaching, and he had more to do with his time than to teach a raw beginner with conscientious scruples and a nervous disposition, but there seemed to be no way out. 'I'll be needing your help over the guns,' he said, 'so I suppose I can't grudge you a little help in qualifying for your legacy. Well, the sooner we get started the sooner we can get back to work. And you'll need time to get the skins cured. You'll need at least three skins for the most minimal bikini.'

77

She looked at him along her long nose. 'I am not turning out in a bikini,' she said firmly.

'You've nothing to be ashamed of in your figure.'

'It's a church service. I want a proper dress. I'll get it, too. I can be very determined.'

'I'm sure of it,' Keith said. 'Is Bert Hayes in charge of Mr Grass's guns? Get him on the house-phone for me, please.'

While he waited, Keith considered the advantage of starting her off with a two-two rifle. It would be the more suitable weapon for rabbits in summer, he thought, but the idea of letting a novice loose with a weapon that could kill at a mile was unappealing.

NINE

Before they left for their promised visit to the police, Keith had a few minutes in which to discover that, for all her vacillation in the face of her ethical doubts, Miss Wyper was not one to be bested by any mere contrivance. She showed an immediate grasp of the basic rules of safety – better by far than the general had managed in half a century – and, after Keith had made a temporary adjustment for her by building up the comb with layers of adhesive tape, she managed to knock a turnip off a fence-post and then to hit it again when it was bowled across the grass in front of her.

At the door, Roach handed him the general's gun. As soon as the door closed Keith, as an automatic gesture, slipped the gun out of its bag and dropped the barrels to check their emptiness. They were freshly cleaned. He stowed the gun in the boot of the Rolls.

The big car, with Bert Hayes at the wheel, made light work of the thirty-mile journey.

If Mr Enterkin had not taken Keith to meet Inspector Glynder, or the inspector had not received them with such a predisposition for dislike, or even if the two visitors had not still been in a mild glow from a vinous lunch, the true explanation of Mr Grass's death might never have emerged. But the inspector, an intelligent and efficient officer in all other respects, was not without his blind spots, and it was unfortunate that the virtues of his visitors were obscured by no less than three of them. The inspector was city reared, and his service with a predominantly rural force had not moderated his belief that the shotgun was an instrument of criminals and butchers. His experience of lawyers had led him to damn the whole profession as being dedicated to securing the acquittal of the guilty. And he saw the forthcoming memorial service as a flagrant breach of the peace. He chose to open the discussion on the last subject.

Enterkin's visit was aimed at no more than the collection of certain of Mr Grass's property still in police hands and giving Keith a chance to enquire into circumstances surrounding his death. Enterkin was aware by now of the dislike and mistrust in which the inspector was held by the shooting community and he was offended by the distaste on the inspector's face as, guardedly, they shook hands. The matters of the leases of certain police premises, and the legality of the memorial service, had been discussed long since and at much higher level, so that Enterkin was in no mood to listen to a lengthy tirade, half plea and half threats, aimed at inducing him to modify or even to abandon the service.

The solicitor half-listened, but his real mind strayed. Perhaps it was an aftermath of his long sessions with Mr Grass over the will, but a touch of the late gentleman's philosophy was laying wanton hands on him and for a moment he toyed with the idea of interrupting the inspector. "By the way," he would say, "umpty pounds were left to you —" the exact figure would require delicacy of judgment "— on condition that you attend the service and lead the congregation in a rousing chorus of 'For he was a jolly good fellow'. You are to be dressed as a member of the Greek Guard, and to ride a donkey which will be provided out of the executry." The inspector seemed impoverished and none to happy about it. Five hundred pounds, give or take a few, would almost certainly persuade him. Even if the amount were lost from his own fee . . .

Mr Enterkin pulled himself together, and sighed. Then, finding that his sigh had caught the inspector's attention, he broke in. 'My duty,' he said, 'is to enable the beneficiaries to qualify for their legacies, provided that there are, in *my* opinion, no infractions of the law. You and I may have differing opinions as to what may constitute a breach of the peace or conduct likely to cause it. But I am quite sure that your superiors have made it clear to you that any rash interference on your part will not only cost police charities some very large bequests but will leave your force in acute difficulties when your leases of certain properties run out over the next few years. If you intervene, Inspector, unless *I* have called you, you will have your head in a sling. Is that quite clear?'

Inspector Glynder's face, triangular over a thin, blue jaw, reddened and he pursed thin lips. 'Quite clear,' he said slowly. 'The position seems to be as you state it. But I'll warn you right now that if you let things get out of hand and do *not* call me, I'll see to the prosecution of all offenders, including you personally.'

The two men glared at each other. Enterkin was remembering a contingency sum, hidden in the will, which enabled him to disburse money, at his own sole discretion, if needed to ensure the success of the service. He wondered how far the inspector could be pushed by a thousand pounds.

Keith, meanwhile, was quite unaware that the inspector held him in almost equal disdain and was horrified at the hostilities. 'Could we get on?' he asked. 'We came over to recover any of Mr Grass's property still in your hands.'

Inspector Glynder seemed to draw relief from the change of subject. He spoke briefly into an internal telephone. 'I asked for his bits and pieces to be brought over here. Though I don't know why you should bother, except for the cash. He had almost a hundred and fifty pounds on him.'

A uniformed constable entered, deposited a shotgun and a large cardboard carton on the inspector's desk, and departed.

Keith picked up the gun and broke it open. It was unloaded. He looked through the barrels. The left had been fired but the right was clean. 'You haven't minded his things very well,' he said. 'This gun's all rusty.'

The inspector bristled again. 'It's only an old gun.'

Enterkin probed for a weakness. 'What would you put it's value at, Inspector?' he asked.

Glynder sensed danger, but it was too late to draw back. 'About fifty pounds,' he said.

Keith had to smile. 'This is a Churchill Premier,' he said. 'The pair, in good order, would fetch over six thousand.'

'And,' Enterkin said, 'if you or your subordinates have reduced its value by negligence, you'll have a lawsuit on your hands.'

'It was hardly our responsibility that the gun was left lying out overnight,' the inspector said angrily.

'It seems to have been kept in a damp place ever since,' Keith said. 'But I dare say it'll clean up. Did your men unload it?'

'Of course. It would hardly have been safe to carry it around and into the inquiry still loaded. It was as you'd expect, a live cartridge in the right barrel and an empty one in the left.'

Out of the carton the inspector lifted a pair of light but strong hand-made leather boots, followed by some clothing in a polythene bag. Through the plastic, heavy bloodstains could be seen on the clothes.

Keith and Mr Enterkin stood up and looked down into the box, to the inspector's displeasure. Keith saw a cartridge-belt with two empty pockets, and a miscellany of smaller items. Enterkin picked up a watch. 'You realise,' he said, 'that this is just about the most expensive make of wrist-watch in the world?'

The inspector made a sound which could have been interpreted either way. Enterkin prepared to needle the inspector at length over his failure to recognise value when he saw it, but Keith's eye was caught by something else in the box. He picked it up. 'What's this?'

The inspector snatched it out of his hand. 'Do you mind? This shouldn't have come over with the rest. It is evidence, not property – the shot and so on which the pathologist recovered from the body.'

'I'd like to see it, please,' Keith said.

'I don't think –'

'If you have closed the case,' Enterkin said, 'then it is no longer evidence. And if it came from Mr Grass's own gun, then it was his property and reverts to his estate.'

'But it has no value!'

Keith was becoming as irritated with the inspector as was the solicitor. 'Lead shot is an expensive commodity,' Keith said.

'How would you like me to apply for a court order?' Enterkin asked.

Inspector Glynder hesitated, grimaced and then almost threw the small bag at Keith. Keith looked at it for a few seconds, and stood very still. Out of the cardboard box he took the fired and the unfired cartridges and he helped himself to a small magnifier from the inspector's desk. 'How do you see the accident?' he asked.

The inspector sat up straighter, a little of his self-importance restored. 'The body was lying on its back, feet towards the fence. Do you know the place?'

'I've seen it.'

'Then you know that there was a bank beyond the fence, and a path down the bank at that very point. We found the gun about ten yards down the bank, with its muzzles pointing up towards where the body was lying. Clear so far?'

Enterkin said, 'You forgot to ask him whether he was sitting comfortably.'

'Quite clear,' Keith said hastily. The inspector's manner might be patronising, but he wanted the rest of the story.

The inspector glared at Enterkin, but went on. 'The only explanation to fit the facts was that Mr Grass had been climbing the fence with his gun in one hand and slipped or started to lose his balance. The gun went out of his hands and landed on the path. It may have bounced or slid some way before it went off – if there were any marks, the over-night snow obscured them. Mr Grass, seeing the danger, threw up his hands to guard his face, with the result that his hands as well as his head were badly damaged.'

'Making identification very difficult?'

'That's a fact. There was no doubt about the clothing, of course, but, in view of the value of the estate and the importance of the man, the courts, the lawyers,' with a glare which Enterkin absorbed with signs of amusement, 'and the insurance companies were insistent on identification of the body itself. In the end, they accepted a combination of medical and dental evidence, together with the print of a naked foot from the polished floor of his wardrobe.'

'Rather an unlikely sort of mishap, wouldn't you say?'

The inspector, who had started to relax, tautened up again. He transferred his visible hatred from Enterkin to Keith. 'Nothing unlikely about it,' he said. 'People are careless with guns every day of the week.'

Keith decided to ignore the sweeping condemnation. 'Mr Grass was careful, not to say fussy, with guns,' he said.

'They can all slip from time to time – especially a man who carries a flask.' The inspector took a large silver flask out of the carton.

Enterkin took it out of his hand and examined it. 'Whatever kind of reputation he had, it wasn't as much of a drinker. You had this tested?'

'As a matter of routine, yes. It contains neat whisky.'

'Nothing else?'

'Nothing that we could detect.'

Enterkin unscrewed two silver cups from the cap of the flask. 'As executor, I think I'm entitled to take a sample. Purely to test the quality, of course. Would you care to join me, Inspector? I'd appreciate a second opinion.'

The offer was well meant but badly received. The inspector shook his head angrily. The solicitor, who had meant the offer as an olive branch, hardened his heart. 'You, Keith?' he asked.

Keith looked up from the magnifier. 'In my capacity as human guinea-pig, just in case the analysts didn't look for the right poison, why not?'

Enterkin poured the second cup for Keith and sat back. As he sipped the excellent malt, the solicitor's mind strayed again. He enjoyed a brief mental picture of the inspector attending the memorial service on a hand-cart as half of a tableau re-creating Rodin's famous statue "The Kiss". He would be partnered with one of the older of the female legatees, and the pair would be attired in long woollen combinations.

Keith tossed his whisky off and put the silver cup down on the inspector's desk. Enterkin refilled it.

'I'm sorry, Inspector,' Keith said, 'but that explanation of Mr Grass's death just won't wash.'

Inspector Glynder got to his feet and glared over their

heads. 'I am also sorry,' he said. 'But I have had enough of the pair of you, sitting in my office drinking and trying to stir up trouble. You had better go now, before I lose patience altogether. And take your precious rubbish with you.'

Keith was honestly surprised. He had been aware of a slight friction between the two branches of the law, but, insulated as he was by lunchtime wine topped up with whisky, he had thought that he and the inspector were having no more than a friendly chat. 'I think you should listen,' he said gently. 'If you don't, you'll end up with egg all over your face, because I'll take the matter a whole lot further. I'm not saying that there wasn't an accident, but, if there was, then somebody tampered with the evidence to make it look like foul play.'

Inspector Glynder sat down suddenly. 'Why would anybody do that?'

Keith shrugged. 'To cover up his own negligence, perhaps,' he suggested.

Enterkin opened his mouth, and then closed it again.

'Evidence?' the inspector asked at last.

'I take it that you didn't get any expert ballistical advice?'

'Why the hell should we?' the inspector asked angrily. 'It was a plain enquiry into an self-evident fatal accident, not a criminal investigation. And you can't match shot to a gun as you can a bullet.'

'All the same, you can match shot to a cartridge, and a cartridge to a gun. And this cartridge,' Keith held up the spent cartridge, 'did not fire the contents of that envelope.'

The inspector sat quietly, very much on his guard, but Enterkin gave a grunt. Keith paused for a moment, marshalling his thoughts. He found that he had emptied the silver cup. He recaptured the flask from Enterkin and refilled it. This really was excellent whisky.

Keith held up the two cartridges. 'These are both Eley Grand Prix. They're both stamped as containing Number Six shot, which would be normal for small-game shooting.' He handed the two cartridges to the inspector, took a sip and went on. 'You may like to compare them. One has been fired, of course, so it's open at one end. But if you look at the brass end you'll see that apart from the small dent made by the firing-pin they're virtually identical. This means that the cartridge has never been reloaded. When you reload a cartridge you have to force a re-sizing die onto it, because it was expanded by pressure when it was fired. It leaves a slightly different contour just above the rim.'

'Nobody ever suggested that it had been reloaded,' said Glynder.

'No. But without even opening your little envelope I could see that, along with the shot, the pathologist recovered a plastic wad. Wads quite often do penetrate the target of a close-range shot. Plastic wads like that are used in some cartridges, mostly for clay pigeon shooting, and they're widely sold to those who reload their own. But they are not used in the Grand Prix.'

'They might both have been reloaded,' the inspector said.

Keith shook his head. 'No. It's one of the things you learn to recognise. I load my own, and I know that if it's a reload it's Number Six, and if it's straight from a manufacturer then it's whatever size is printed on it. Those were both straight out of the box. Here's one of the general's reloads, if you want to compare it.' Keith took a cartridge from his pocket and handed it over.

While Inspector Glynder pored over the three cartridges, Keith picked up the silver cup. It seemed to be empty again, but then, it was ridiculously small. He held it out to Enterkin who had taken fresh possession of the flask.

After a minute, the inspector sighed. 'You're saying that the wad removed from Mr Grass's head could not have come from the empty cartridge in his gun. Is that a fair summary?'

'It is.'

'The cartridge which killed him was a reloaded one? You said that these wads are used in other cartridges.'

'It was a reload,' Keith said. 'Definitely.' He poured some of the tiny pellets into his palm. The inspector looked unhappy but made no protest. 'This shot is home-made. It varies slightly in size. And there seems to be a tiny dimple in each one, which is typical.'

'Thank you for your –'

'An analyst could give you a good indication as to whether the original lead had come from old battery-plates, lead pipe, roofing lead, printer's metal, spent bullets or what-the-hell, and that might give you a further lead.'

'It might, might it?'

Enterkin saw the danger signals and was content with an internal smile that never showed on his round and innocent face. Keith was away in a world of his own. 'As far as I know,' he said, 'there's only one man pouring shot around here, and that's Joe Merson the poacher. I'll ask around for you and see if I can find out if anyone else pours shot. Merson's away just now, but you could look in his place and get samples. Of course, his mixture may change from time to time, depending on where his lead supplies come from. The trouble is that cartridges get passed from hand to hand. Somebody running short borrows a few. Even if he doesn't use them, he may repay the loan with a random selection out of his bag. What we've got to do –'

A man can only stand just so much of seeing his job done for him, and even less of being shown that he has slipped up badly. The inspector broke in so loudly that Keith was blasted into silence. 'Are you absolutely sure of all this? The wad, and so on?'

'Absolutely. Look, I've got an unused Grand Prix here. I'll just cut it open and show you –'

'No … you … will … *not!*' If the inspector was ungracious, he might well be forgiven. He was not looking forward to reporting these developments. 'There has been more than enough meddling with the evidence. Our experts can take it from here. You will kindly leave everything behind you and go.'

Keith was almost dumbstruck at the ingratitude, as he saw it. 'Is that all the thanks I get?' he demanded.

Enterkin looked from one to the other and laughed until his jowls shook, his belly wobbled and tears hopped down his cheeks. 'Come away, Keith,' he said at last. 'I don't think you're getting any thanks at all.'

TEN

As the big car wafted them back towards Whinkirk and Keith imagined himself boiling Inspector Glynder in oil, Enterkin gradually brought his chuckles under control. 'An excellent week's work,' he said at last.

'We've only been here a day and a bit,' Keith pointed out, 'and I've hardly even glimpsed the guns.'

'A good week's work all the same.' Enterkin dried his eyes and became serious. 'If you don't do another hand's turn until Monday, you've earned your fee for the week.'

'Why are you so pleased? Surely the fact that your client didn't die in a simple accident will only make a lot of stramash and complicate your life for you.'

Enterkin shook his head. 'It'll simplify it no end. No doubt your revelations will be a disaster for somebody. Offhand I can think of several, including the perpetrator of whatever crime was committed, several insurance brokers – and Inspector Glynder, who will have one hell of a lot of explaining to do.'

'Insurance brokers?'

'Yes.' Enterkin's chubby face lit up in smiles again. 'I refrained from telling you what we wanted because your evidence, if the matter should come to court, will carry more weight if you can honestly state that you came to your conclusions with minimal prompting. However, I can now tell you that your discoveries may well save the executry from total disaster.'

'The trust's all right isn't it?' Keith asked anxiously.

'I hope so. But as residuary legatee it gets what's left over after the beneficiaries and the taxman have had their whack. To cover the tax liability, Mr Grass took out several enormous insurance policies. But he took them out shortly after General Springburn – er – peppered him, I think, is the expression. The insurers called for medical reports, took note of the incident and insisted on a qualification that excluded accidents while shooting.'

'But if he was murdered, they still pay up?'

'Certainly.'

'But suppose he was murdered by one of the beneficiaries.'

'Same answer, except that that particular beneficiary would be debarred from inheriting. You had me worried when you pointed to the possibility that somebody had tampered with the evidence in order to cover up their own negligence. Unlikely, though.'

'I was only trying to offer Glynder a face-saver. How do you like that petty-minded dreip, though? If I hadn't pushed him, he'd have hushed the whole thing up.'

'I'll tell you something,' Enterkin said. 'While you and he were having your little altercation, I was wrestling with temptation. I was sorely tempted to manufacture a fictitious legacy for the inspector. He struck me as a man that'd do anything for a thousand or two. Such as coming to the service as Lady Godiva, in a long wig, flesh-coloured body-stocking and suitable padding, mounted on one of Mr Grass's horses.'

'For the pleasure of seeing that,' Keith said, 'I'd chip in half the legacy.'

'Would you really?'

Keith realised in time that he was talking about a large sum of money. 'Not really,' he said. 'I'll tell you what, though. I'll make you my offer when I've seen all the guns, and if you care to accept a lower figure I'll kick the balance back to you as a secret fund for the inspector's legacy. How does that sound?'

'Musical. My boy, you have a twisted mind. What a lawyer you'd have made! But no,' Mr Enterkin said wistfully. 'It was just the whisky doing my thinking for me. Sober, I wouldn't think of such a thing.'

'Pity, though.'

'It is indeed,' Mr Enterkin said with a sigh.

Keith would have preferred a return to Whinkirk House, but Mr Enterkin was adamant that they be driven to the inn. He had some telephoning to do, he said, and there was more confidentiality to be obtained by borrowing Harvey Brown's tiny office than at Whinkirk House where all the many telephones shared a common line.

'All right, then,' Keith said as they entered the village. 'I'll take the car on and walk back.'

Mr Enterkin shook his head.

'But I haven't had more than a glance at the guns yet.'

'And if you get in among them today, you'll take root. I'll probably want to consult you after I've done my telephoning, or even during it, and I don't want to hang about.'

'You're just afraid that I'll keep you waiting for your dinner.'

'You couldn't,' Mr Enterkin said. 'I'm dining out.'

'Who with?'

'Never you mind. Surely a lawyer has a right to some confidentiality.'

'Or secretiveness,' Keith said. A tiny thought almost germinated, but their arrival at the inn blew the seed away.

Harvey Brown was opening the bars as they came in. Mr Enterkin begged the use of the office and disappeared.

Brutus planted himself in front of the empty fireplace. Keith took a stool.

'The usual?' Harvey asked.

Keith made a face. His stomach was sending messages on the subject of irregular drinking habits. 'A pint of shandy,' he said, 'and just a dash of feminine company. No luscious barmaid this evening?'

'She begged the evening off.' (Once again the penny almost dropped.) 'Am I not good-looking enough for you?' Harvey Brown's face had been ugly even before rival boxers had broken his nose and raised lumps which nature had omitted, but he had a charming smile.

'Not by a mile,' Keith said. 'Have one with me.' They chatted in ribald style, as men will, until Mr Enterkin came back.

The solicitor was looking harrassed. He led Keith away from the bar to a corner table. 'Pussy was already among the pigeons,' he said, 'but now there's a change of roles. The various solicitors acting for the estate, in league with the tax authorities, are now the cat, and the underwriters are the pigeon and overdue for plucking. I'll have to get down to London early tomorrow for a meeting that may run on through another day or two. Do you want to stay here or go home?'

'Could I take a few of the guns home with me to appraise and overhaul?'

'I don't see why not. I'll give Miss Wyper a ring and tell her to look out a selection, together with their papers. Would you do me the favour of looking after this smelly tyke for me? You can come to Renfrew and see me off on the shuttle in the morning, and then take the car on to Newton Launder.'

'Yes, of course I'll take Brutus,' Keith said. 'But send the car back for me. I could use the morning here.'

'Suit yourself, my boy, suit yourself. We'll confer at the weekend with a view to returning here next Monday. Well, I must away. You'll oblige me by spending the evening writing out a precognition – you know the style.' And Mr Enterkin bounced to his feet and left the room, whistling.

'I can't think what he's so chirpy about,' Keith said.

'Humph!' said Harvey Brown.

Keith went to phone Molly.

When Mr Enterkin presented himself at Penny Laing's door that evening and was invited inside there was a shyness between them, not at their lovemaking of the night before, because the age was liberated although their generation had come late to it, but because of its almost explosive haste. Each had grown up in the belief that, while such affairs might occur, they were preceded by a lengthy, ritual court-ship. Now that the first novelty had rubbed off their attraction for each other, each was afraid of having lost the other's respect.

They remained standing for a moment in the shadowed interior, which smelled fresh and yet old-fashioned. Polish and lavender, Mr Enterkin decided.

'That was a load of old rubbish you told me last night,' she said suddenly. She chuckled. 'Properly had me going, you did!'

It came back to Mr Enterkin that her first attraction for him had been her voice and its gentle country accent. He laughed, and the tension between them was gone. 'Yes,' he said. 'My tongue ran away with me. I said all that a fat old man could say without making himself ridiculous. If I had told you what I felt already, it would have sounded like the same old line that men give to women whether they mean it

94

or not. But now I can tell you the truth. The reason why the sun has been shining all day was because I was going to see you again.'

'I've been looking forward too,' she said. They moved closer together. 'You're not so old. And if I don't go on a diet soon, I'll make two of you.'

Mr Enterkin chose to ignore the fact that she was taller than he by several inches. 'Don't diet on my account,' he said fondly. 'Nothing so delectable should be dispensed in niggardly portions.' His words reminded him of another need. 'If only you could cook . . .'

'Ah, I've no fears on that score. And I can take a hint.' She gave him a gentle push. 'No need to hurry me, I've the whole evening off.'

The food, if not as sumptuous as Mrs Roach's, was delicious, and the portions were far from niggardly. Between mouthfuls, he said, 'You must hear all the gossip in the bar?'

She nodded. 'I can't help but hear. They – they were talking about us at lunchtime. I wasn't meant to hear it, but I did. I was seen leaving the inn. At first they thought it was your friend I'd been with.'

Mr Enterkin was a little piqued that Keith should have stolen his thunder, but he put it behind him. 'Do you mind them guessing about us?' he asked.

She considered the question. 'Not as long as you don't,' she said. 'If you were ashamed, then I would be too.'

'Ashamed? If it weren't for your sake I'd put an advertisement in *The Times*, proclaiming my triumph to the world. But that wasn't what I meant to ask about. What did the village gossip make of Mr Grass's death?'

'Well. At first there was some that thought he was up to one of his jokes but that he'd gone a bit too far this time and he'd get himself into real trouble that he couldn't buy his way out of. But there was only one or two thought that, and soon they all accepted that he was dead, and there was one or two said that he'd been done in.'

Mr Enterkin put down his knife and fork. 'That was delicious. Quite delicious. Why yes, if there's any left . . . Was there any comment about Joe Merson vanishing at the same time?'

'Yes. But then there was a lot of foolishness talked. Joe's always going off, poaching or thieving. Once he got caught, up in Aberdeenshire, and went inside for six months under some other name. And then Harry Pratt — he's our local Bobby — said as he'd seen old Joe in the 'phone box outside the post office, a couple of days after Mr Grass got shot, so they forgot about it. There was plenty else to talk about, like whether Mr Grass was murdered.'

'Who was first favourite for the culprit?'

'You mean the murderer?' She shivered, not unpleasurably. 'Sounds awful when you say it like that. Makes it sort of real and evil. Mind you, it was nearly all just talk, and only a few of them carried on about it. But some was for blaming Joe Merson, and some said it was old Bert Yates (because him and Mr Grass was about at daggers drawn) and somebody else said it'd surely be an angry husband, and there was plenty of names suggested but not seriously. Then they heard about the legacies, and everything said after that was just in fun. Every time the news got out that somebody had something coming there'd be suggestions about what he'd do with it or she'd done for it. All kinds of fanciful things were thought up, you know how people are.' (Mr Enterkin nodded thoughtfully. His mouth was full.) 'And then word got round about the memorial service and the things people have got to do, and they've not talked about much else since.'

They did they washing-up together — a chore of which Mr

Enterkin, the confirmed bachelor, had become heartily sick, but which he found a pleasure, almost a game, when shared with an attractive woman in flirtatious mood. Then they sat on the couch and held hands.

'I've got to go up to London tomorrow,' Enterkin said at last.

'Will you be back before the weekend?'

He was tempted, but he stood firm. 'I'd better get back and clear my desk,' he said. 'I'd rather be here, but duty calls. I'll see you without fail on Monday.'

He had thought that, after spending himself with such prodigality the night before, it would be a few days before he could rouse the devil again. He had reckoned without the effects of previous celibacy, good food and the singular effect that Penny's plump charms had on his elderly hormones. It was fortunate that he had taken the precaution of obtaining a key to the inn.

ELEVEN

In the morning, while Mr Enterkin was being carried to Renfrew Airport in a comfort and dignity to which he would dearly have liked to become acustomed, Keith and Brutus set off again. One of Keith's objectives was to learn a little more about the lie of the estate, so he chose a fresh route. It had rained in the night, to the relief of the farmers, but the sun was out again. Brutus pranced beside him, happy that Keith was happy, glad to be walking again, puzzled that his instincts impelled him towards actions that he did not understand.

They were half-way to Winter's cottage when a macintoshed figure stepped out of a bush. Miss Wyper was carrying Mr Grass's Darne, the sliding breech open as custom demanded. 'Any luck?' Keith asked.

'Nothing.' She sounded depressed. 'I never find them sitting, and when they run they're too quick for me.'

'And all the while, you're scaring them into cover,' Keith said. He sighed. His morning was in danger of going up the spout. 'We'll walk on, not by the way you've been. You'd have more chance at dawn or dusk, but they may be sitting out taking the sun. The trick is to walk very quietly through cover and then to peep out at the far end.'

They followed a ride across the middle of a small wood, past a release-pen waiting for the new broods of pheasant poults. They walked very softly with Brutus, resentful but curious, at heel. Keith put his mouth close to Miss Wyper's ear. 'Go forward gently and look both ways.'

His advice was good. A rabbit was sitting up, thirty yards

away. She fired, and it toppled. Instantly, another bolted almost from underfoot and Keith bowled it over in the open and then swung up to catch a startled woodpigeon that clattered out of the branches overhead and kill it dead in the air.

It was a moment of earthy triumph.

Miss Wyper would have run forward but he stopped her. A rabbit with a kick left in it may teach a dog to be hard-mouthed, so he waited a full minute and then sent Brutus. The rabbits resembled the dummies of his training and he brought them to hand at once. Then, to Keith's delight, he went for the pigeon, lifted it gently but firmly and fetched it back, pride in achievement shining around him.

If Keith was delighted, Miss Wyper was overwhelmed. This was her first introduction to the truly fulfilled dog, the working dog doing the job for which it was bred. Just as Brutus had experienced a revelation of his purpose in life, she, as a woolly minded doggy-lover, caught a first glimpse of the true relationship between man and dog.

Brutus accepted their praises as being no more than his due, but within his black frame great emotions were stirring. From now on he was to be a devotee, an addict, a fanatic. Keith could read the signs, but there was nothing to tell him that this new enthusiasm was soon to become crucial to his own survival.

Alice Wyper, however, was less enthusiastic about receiving her furry victim. Shrinking back with a small squeal, she said that she couldn't, she just couldn't.

'Bill would want you to,' Keith pointed out, but she shuddered and shook her head. 'For ten thousand quid?' She put her hand out and drew it away again. 'Why not, for God's sake?'

'It's still warm. If it wriggled, I think I'd die.'

99

'Look, if it wriggles I promise I'll die too.'

'I can't be sure.'

Keith sighed. He seemed to be doing a lot of sighing around Miss Wyper. Using his pen-knife, he paunched the two rabbits and passed the left leg of each through the right. 'If it moves again,' he said, 'I'll come round to believing in universal resurrection.'

Miss Wyper, green but determined, picked up her bunny by the back legs, using two fingers. 'Can't I put it in your bag?' she asked.

Their relationship, Keith thought, was becoming more and more like something dreamed up by D. H. Lawrence in fevered mood, but he was not inclined to exploit it in a damp wood with midges dancing in the sunlight. Besides, he would be with Molly soon. 'You're going to have to skin it,' he reminded her.

'Of course,' she said disdainfully.

They followed a thick hedge to another ride where feed-hoppers had been set up in readiness; out of that wood and into a small spinney. There was a sudden eruption under their feet. A furious cock pheasant exploded into the air, something white shrouding its head. Blind and angry, it screeched and beat its wings against the undergrowth until it shook off its blindfold and soared on blurring wings, up into the sunlight. A small hen pheasant had fallen foul of the same trick but was taking it more passively, crouching in the grass and only rushing blindly away from their footsteps. In the end, Brutus retrieved the bird unhurt. Keith gently removed the paper.

'Look at this,' he said. 'An old poacher's trick. A paper cone with something sticky and tasty inside – in this case, treacle and raisins. I suppose our poacher's away by now, with us blasting off in the next field, but we'd better get rid of these things.'

They searched, but the little cones were hard to find in the grass. Brutus' long nose, a thousand times more sensitive than that of a man, had already identified the other visitor to the spinney and soon searched out another five of the cones. Brutus ate them, paper and all.

While Alice Wyper, with all the concentration of a surgeon, skinned her rabbit in Mrs Winter's kitchen and under that lady's kind but firm direction, Keith found Winter out at the pheasant pens and made the acquaintance of his two sons, a pair of enormous but inarticulate youths who faded quietly into the background as soon as attention was removed from them.

'I meant to ask you about the local rules,' Keith said.

Winter nodded. 'I just thought I'd wait and watch you,' he said. 'Mostly, the rules are just common-sense and good behaviour and you've been complying with them.' (Keith nodded in acknowledgement of what he recognised as high praise.) 'There's just one more thing. You will pick up your cartridges and take them home with you. I will not abide spent cases left lying. We had a young bullock killed last year by swallowing one. Stupid beast! It did a lot of damage to relationships with the farmers.'

Keith nodded humbly. 'I don't know what vermin you want taken and what left,' he said.

'Aye. You'll not shoot down by the loch while the duck are breeding, but if you see any evidence of predators down yonder you'll tip me the wink. The loons can aye set traps. I ken you'll not shoot at birds of prey – I saw you let a wind-hover go by. But if you can get a crack at a carrion crow or a magpie, tak' it, there's o'er many of the buggers come in from beyond the march. Leave stoats and weasels to me – I like to have just enough about the place to keep the rats down. Now, come awa' in and see the map.'

A large map was hanging on the parlour wall, protected by a sheet of perspex which was scrawled with notes and arrows. The estate, Keith saw, was shaped much like a human left ear, about two miles wide and rather more in length. At the southern end, just above the lobe, was a lake of about thirty acres. The village was strung out along part of the eastern edge. Whinkirk House occupied a position corresponding to the tragus of the ear. Other houses were strung out around the perimeter, backed by the solid woodland that occupied the higher ground and sheltered the estate. The rest was farmland, laced by the many coverts and dotted with occasional cottages or groups of farm-buildings.

Winter laid his finger on a red star drawn on the perspex. 'You'll oblige me by giving this corner the go-by,' he said. 'There's a Dusky Thrush nesting there, a great rarity. Maybe you could get your wife to come and take its photo? We've rigged a wee hide.'

'Maybe I could,' Keith said absently. While he spoke, he was memorising the features and boundaries and the locations and ownerships of the buildings. 'And we'd better tell Miss Wyper things like to keep moving and not to linger in the one place and unsettle your birds.'

'What *is* this about her?' Winter asked plaintively. 'Yon lawyer-mannie you was wi', he phoned me and said she was to be allowed to shoot coneys. Well, I knew fine that she'd never do that, there was more chance of her coming naked into the kirk, the way she feels.'

'Funny you should say that. With her, it's the one or the other.' He explained to Winter the terms of Miss Wyper's legacy.

To Keith's surprise, the dour keeper let go a shout of laughter. 'You canna' help but hand it to the man,' he said.

'Most of the terms and conditions in his will sound daft, but there's aye a degree of wisdom behind them. Miss Wyper, now. If she's helped over her prejudices she'll be that much happier in her work here.'

Winter's view was the exact opposite of that expressed by the general's daughter, but Keith was beginning to agree with the keeper. 'I gave her as much advice as I thought she could absorb,' he said. 'But you'd better take her in hand. And if you see her coming, either wave a red flag or get your head down.'

'Maybe I'll take to wearing a white macintosh,' Winter suggested.

'I don't think she's likely to be as dangerous as the general.' Mention of dangerous behaviour reminded Keith of something else. 'By the bye, do I remember Mr Roach saying that Mr Grass's other dog got shot during the winter?'

'That wisna' carelessness with a gun. Carelessness with the dog, maybe. Mr Yates at North Farm shot her. Worrying sheep, he said. Now, I dinna' ken the facts of the matter and I didna' see the corpus. He said as he never recognised the dog, and the one spaniel can look awful like another, except maybe to its owner. They say there was wool between its teeth. Mr Grass was a bittie unreasonable but, as he said, it's no' unknown for a farmer to put a wee bit wool in the dog's mouth after the event.'

'Spaniels don't start sheep-chasing unless another dog leads them into it,' Keith said.

'Aye. That's what Mr Grass said. And Yates himself has a half-bred collie with a good bit of the devil in him, and he was out that night, so they say, although he lives most of his life on a chain, being o'er wild.' They were still standing in front of the map, and Winter shuffled his feet uncomfortably. 'They say that Mulberry ran off from outside a certain lady's house. She was a good young bitch, too, and coming along well.'

'Mulberry was?'

'Aye, Mulberry. I reckon that's why old Yates wants to see either you or yon lawyer mannie. He'll be anxious to ken that the will says nothing about ending his tenancy. Mr Grass was having a blue fit, right up to the day he died.'

'I'll find out,' Keith promised, 'and pay him a call. You wouldn't care to tell me which lady's house was rumoured to be the one that Mulberry ran off from?'

'I wouldn't care to bandy a lady's name,' Winter said carefully. 'But you canna' bandy a house, now can you? When you come to the one with the yellow paint, the lady'll not be very far awa'.'

Shortly thereafter, Miss Wyper emerged from the kitchen and gave the keeper a nervous greeting. However, instead of seeking revenge for past arguments, Winter smiled and nodded and enquired after her progress with the skinning-knife.

Miss Wyper, who was still looking pale and distraught, shuddered in a ladylike manner. 'I managed it,' she said. 'Mrs Winter said that I did it very well. But I'm not sure that I could do it again.'

'You'll be a sensation if you don't,' Keith pointed out. 'I'd better be on my way. Good hunting!'

'Time that I was moving and a',' Winter said. He came to the door with Keith and took his own gun down from a pair of hooks above the coat-rack.

'I see you like a repeater,' Keith said.

'Not to say like. It's handy for five quick shots when you're among the vermin, and a damned pest when you're searching the brambles for five empty cartridges. It's no' everybody's choice. The general was trying one earlier in the year, and he couldn't get along with it at all.'

Keith set off again. He had hoped further to advance the training of Brutus, but the pigeon were elusive and to settle down in one place to shoot would have disturbed the nesting gamebirds. He reached the general's house with still only one bird in the bag.

There was a delay before the general answered the bell. He took Keith inside, leaving Brutus and his own cocker spaniels in the garden.

'I've brought your gun back,' Keith said, 'with many thanks for the loan. I'm away home until next week and I'll fetch my own gun back with me. Yours needs a clean, but I hadn't any tackle at the inn.'

'Quite all right. No problem. Come through.' The general led him into the gun-room. 'Drink?'

'I could use a beer,' Keith said.

'So could I. Get some. Fridge.'

At that particular combination of ideas, Keith'd bladder began to send him urgent messages. 'Perhaps I could pay a call while you do your fetching?' he suggested.

'Call? Oh, yes. Of course. This way.'

Coming out of the general's dark cloakroom into a darker passage, Keith was aware of a draught and a sudden flood of light as the general opened a door from a sunlit kitchen. Juggling a tray of bottles and glasses, the general closed the door carefully behind him.

They had a beer together in the gunroom and chatted for a few minutes. The general seemed nervous. His voice and gestures, always larger than life, were larger still and he seemed relieved to escort Keith to the front door and fling it open.

Brutus was sitting on the doorstep. The general's two

cockers were standing well back, waiting to enjoy the fun. Brutus was bearing up under the weight of an enormous cock pheasant. He delivered it into Keith's hand. Keith passed it on to the general.

'From your kitchen, I'm very much afraid,' he said.

The general laughed wildly. 'Frozen. Bought in. Dinner party,' he said. He sounded ready to choke.

In the hope of eradicating, or at least reducing, the memory of the gaffe, Keith stopped a few yards short of the inn and handed Brutus the pigeon. Brutus accepted the, by now, somewhat tatty bird and carried it right into the public bar, showing himself with pride to the assembled drinkers. He was duly made a great fuss of, and rewarded with potato crisps which he ate with great relish all mixed up with pigeon feathers.

TWELVE

Keith and Brutus, after an early lunch, were collected from the inn by Bert Hayes. The Rolls made easy going of a road that twined through hills sometimes wooded, often green, with heather sometimes spilling down from the high ground. Keith passed the time looking out of the car's dark windows at the countryside under the persistent sun, and playing his favourite game of 'If I had the shooting, what would I do here?' By the time that they were descending towards Newton Lauder he had identified eight sites for duckponds, miles of potential grouse-moor and more than he could count of places where only a modicum of work was needed to create habitat for pheasant or partridge or snipe. He heaved a mental sigh for such a waste of natural resources.

Bert Hayes slid open the glass screen as they entered the drive of Briesland House. 'Will you be wanting me again before Monday, sir?'

Keith was tempted to commandeer car and chauffeur and to arrive resplendently at his various appointments. On the other hand, perhaps it would be wise not to give Molly a taste for such luxury. 'I don't suppose so,' he said. 'I can always phone.'

'I thought I might go and stay with my sister in Pentland, and save some petrol.'

It occurred to Keith that a weekend which began on the Wednesday evening was generous to a fault. On the other hand, it was true that two or three days of gardening by Hayes was probably worth less than the fuel for the double journey. 'All right,' he said, 'give me a phone number.'

'My sister isn't on the phone, sir. I'll call you each morning for orders.'

'Very well.'

From the huge boot Keith retrieved his light suitcase and the heavy box of guns which Miss Wyper had packed for him. The car slid silently on its way.

Molly was in the kitchen, working with compulsive energy. Her hands were full and floury. Keith hardly noticed that his kiss found her cheek instead of her mouth, but it did occur to him that she greeted the dog more warmly than she did himself.

'So you did come back,' she said.

'Of course I came back,' Keith said, surprised. 'Why wouldn't I? I'm free for the rest of the week, but I brought some guns back to appraise and work on. And it looks very much as if Ray Grass was murdered.'

Ordinarily Molly would have fizzed with curiosity over such news, but she seemed to have other things on her mind. 'You've been busy, then?'

'Very, but there's still a lot to be done. And what-all's been happening back at the ranch?'

'Not a lot. The shop's been very quiet. There's a Joseph Lang sidelock in for repair. Ronnie's borrowed Tanya for today and he'd like to have her all next week. Jack Waterhouse came by. He says that at that price you can keep the Baker rifle, but he's available to do engraving for you. I can't stand that man,' she added. She reached across the kitchen table for the salt-jar and managed to keep her back to Keith while she spoke again in a small voice. 'I've been sleeping better while you were away. Two of me's enough in one bed, and I'm scared you'll bump my bump when you thrash around. So I've moved your things into the other room. Do you mind?'

'I mind,' Keith said. 'But if it's what you want . . .'

'And you're going back next week?'

'That seems to be the general arrangement. Can you manage without me again?'

'Janet and Wal can manage,' Molly said. 'I've polished off your dog-training thing. Can I come with you?'

'Yes, of course you can. I asked you to come last time. Ralph Enterkin says he's going to stay at the inn again, but I've an invitation to stay in Whinkirk House. Which do you want?'

'The house.'

There was a small silence. 'Well,' Keith said, 'I'd better be getting on.' He went out to fetch the box from a sunshine which seemed to have turned grey.

In the kitchen, Molly bowed her head over the stove. Something seemed to have died. A tear fell into the soup, but, she decided, salt and protein never did soup any harm.

Brutus leaned against her leg. He offered a sympathetic paw.

Mr Enterkin reached his office at noon on the Saturday, and before the Old Kirk clock had chimed that hour – seven minutes late, as was its habit – he was on the telephone to Keith at the shop. 'Why the hell is my office knee-deep in guns?' he demanded.

Keith glanced round. Two customers were in the shop. 'I'm on my own for a wee while,' he said. 'Can I come over in about half an hour?'

'We could meet for lunch.'

'I think you'll find it's confidential,' Keith said. 'I'll come to your office. We can lunch after, if you like.'

'Oh very well,' the solicitor said irritably. His sojourn in the expense-account fleshpots of London had enhanced his enjoyment of the epicurean life, and he had been looking forward to a leisurely hour spent chatting over several gins-and-tonic.

'Your dog's out at Briesland House. He seems to have settled in well with Tanya, but I can go and fetch him if you like.'

'No hurry. Whenever's convenient. I have,' Mr Enterkin admitted, 'rather been enjoying the luxury of *not* having to go walkies all the damn time.'

Keith crossed the square to the solicitor's office well within the promised half-hour, and he found Mr Enterkin glowering in his inner sanctum. The desk was dominated by the box, once the container for a croquet set, in which Miss Wyper had packed the guns. Mr Enterkin, from his customary chair, had to crane his short neck to peer over the top.

'How did the cats-and-pigeons go?' Keith asked, dropping into the client's chair.

The solicitor relaxed, thereby disappearing altogether for the moment. 'Very satisfactorily,' said his voice. 'We started off with the solicitors for the personal estate – that's me – and for the various industrial and commercial interests ranged against the tax authorities and the insurance companies, who had decided to gang up against us and to pick the carcase. I put copies of your precognition around the table. The executors were unanimous in deciding to drag their feet over probate until the question of death could be re-examined. The taxmen changed sides as soon as they realised how much to their advantage it would be if the policies paid off. And the insurance companies were left out on a limb, sticking pins in little wax effigies of you and hoping to hell that the police don't agree with you. Now, tell me why my office is being used as a repository for firearms.'

'Self protection,' Keith said. 'I dumped them in the care of

110

your Miss Wilks as soon as I spotted that something was wrong, so that nobody could suggest that I'd had time to make any substitutions.'

'Wrong?' Enterkin's head popped up again over the box. 'You'd better tell me what you mean. And,' he added hastily, 'spare me your customary erudite lecture with diversions into the history of firearms and the biographies of every gun-maker whose name makes even the most fleeting appearance. Nor do I want my nose rubbed against minis-cule traces visible to your eyes alone. Just tell me what you found wrong.'

Keith was piqued. 'You do like the sound of your own voice, don't you?'

Enterkin pursed his lips in judgment. 'It's not that I like the sound of it,' he said at last, 'it's just that I like what I hear it say. And, even at that, I like it better than I like the sound of yours. So be brief but factual.'

Keith bit back a retort. He should have known better than to bandy words with the solicitor. 'Miss Wyper packed up ten, with their papers. From the receipts and so on, the guns purport to be antiques in virtually mint condition. Three of them are good, and I've kept them for minor polishing. There's a Napoleonic musket in the box that I'm not sure of – it's been converted from flint to percussion and then back again, but I think that the reconversion may have been done in the mid-nineteenth century, for export to some remote jungle where percussion caps were not to be had. But it's invoiced as an original flintlock. The other six –'

'Fakes?'

'One outright fake,' Keith said. 'The rest are a mixter-maxter of old and new, major repairs and replacements, a lot of very fancy engraving to dish up commonplace guns as if they were top-grade, plus adding the names of some

111

makers who'd never have let that sort of rubbish out of the shop. Raymond Grass may have been a whizz as a business-man, and he knew a lot about the history of guns, but he was an amateur when it came to dealing.'

'Or he trusted his buyer too much,' Enterkin said.

'True. I thought at first that I'd be able to tell something from the style of engraving, but when I came to look at it it's all copied out of a rare book on engraving that was published around the time of the Golden Jubilee. I thought I had the only copy in Scotland.'

'If you can't get a clue to his identity from the engraving, is there any clue in the receipts and other provenance?'

Keith shrugged, although it was unlikely that the solicitor, who had relaxed his strained posture, could see him. 'I've no idea,' he said. 'I didn't want to start any speculation by phoning around until I'd had a word with you. But the receipts are mostly in Mr Grass's name, and they're fakes, the whole boiling lot of them. In this day and age it's all too easy to cut the heading off somebody's bill-paper and photocopy it. There's one receipt in there that purports to be mine, but the paper's softer than mine and it doesn't have the number in the top right-hand corner. I suppose he bought something out of the shop, got a genuine receipted bill, painted out the date and the number with that stuff that typists use, stuck the heading on a piece of plain paper and bunged it through a Xerox. The lack of a number's a give-away, but if he'd left the number on it might have been possible to trace him through the original purchase. The writing seems to be in a number of different hands, but if he can engrave like that then he can alter his handwriting. The silver and gold inlay work's damn good too. If he'd come to me, I could have put some honest work his way. Instead, I suppose he'll end up in the slammer.'

'Probably,' said Mr Enterkin's voice. 'Did he get away with very much?'

'On those six guns, on an expenditure of about two hundred and fifty quid and two months work, he pulled in just under ten grand. And there's about another hundred guns in the collection. I know it sounds a lot,' Keith said hastily as Mr Enterkin's eyebrows almost preceded the rest of his face into view, 'but you've got to remember that a collector's item in near-mint condition can fetch well into four figures, sometimes five, but you can buy the rubbish, not exactly for pennies but for a few fivers. Now,' Keith dug a gun out of the box and unwrapped it with tender care, 'take this shotgun.' Mr Enterkin's eyes widened in alarm but Keith went on before he could interrupt. 'It's a double-barrel flintlock. It's been restocked recently, and the wood aged with permanganate and with leather dyes, carefully shaded to simulate years of wear. The unwritten rules require that when you do such drastic work on an old gun you record the fact where it can be seen, like inside the trigger-guard. Lesser repairs or new small components you record where it will show up when the gun's dismantled. But there's no such marking on this fellow. It's been a plain gun in its day, a work-horse. The workmanship's nothing special, but the engraving's all recent and it's been browned and polished afresh. One of the giveaways is the style of the hammers. If you'll take a look?'

Enterkin averted his eyes from the gun which, by now, Keith was brandishing under his nose. 'Under no circumstances,' he said firmly.

Keith hardly heard him. 'On the rib, it says *William Maclauchlan, Edinburgh,* but if Maclauchlan made that gun then Leonardo sculpted garden gnomes. The touch-holes don't even —'

'Shut up,' Mr Enterkin said loudly, and Keith fell silent at last. 'You've done a grand job,' the solicitor said, 'and the estate will cheerfully pay you the value of your time, *less* the value of as much of my time as you waste by forcing on me a lot of technical information which I neither care about nor even understand. If we ever manage to prosecute the perpetrator of the frauds you'll no doubt be called to give evidence, and may God have mercy on the judge. Until then, bottle it up.'

'All right,' Keith said. He could find somebody else to tell it all to. 'Do you want me to examine the rest of the collection?'

'Better not,' Mr Enterkin said after a moment's thought. 'For your own sake. We'll get somebody up from London, somebody whose name doesn't figure on any of the documents and who can't possibly be suspected of complicity. If he confirms that fraud such as you've outlined runs through the whole collection, I may have to call in the police; but although it's a large sum I don't suppose we'll ever see a penny of it again. Water under the bridge. I'm inclined to write it off as errors of judgment on the part of Mr Grass.'

'You're missing a very important point,' Keith said. 'If the late Mr Grass had realised that he'd been ripped off and was threatening to howl for the fuzz, somebody could have had a bloody good motive to knock him off before his voice could be heard.'

Mr Enterkin drew himself up to such a height that for the first time Keith could see the whole of his face. He looked aggrieved. 'I do not miss points,' he said severely. 'I wish the police the best of luck in their endeavours, if they make any, to apprehend Mr Grass's killer. But I have no personal lust for vengeance, and the interests of the executry will be satisfied if it is accepted that he did not die naturally.'

Keith, whose hunter's instinct never let him abandon a trail, was shocked. 'You mean you don't give a fish's tit who killed your client?'

'If I do, it is only out of vulgar curiosity.'

'And I stop investigating that matter?'

'Investigate it all you want, but not at the expense of the estate.'

'If you're getting somebody else to look at the guns – which is fine by me, because you'll be able to believe me when I make a low offer for them – and if I'm not to look into the death except in my own time, it hardly seems worth coming back with you.'

The solicitor compared his watch with the clock on the wall and split the difference. There was still time to save something out of the wreckage of his lunchtime. 'Come and eat,' he said. 'We'll talk about it.'

They skirted the Square in silence, and it was only when they were safely established on stools in the hotel bar with drinks before them and a menu in his hand that Mr Enterkin returned to the subject. 'I want you to come back to Whinkirk House with me,' he said. 'Stay away from the guns until we've had an independant expert list them and record his opinion. And it's not the business of the executor or his agents to detect the murderer. But there's still plenty to do. There are answers required about the estate to which I don't even understand the questions. And then there's the trust. I told you about the trust, didn't I?'

'Several times.'

'It's a lot on my mind,' Mr Enterkin said, without hint of apology. 'You see, part of my task is to inaugurate it. The constitution and rules were already laid down by Mr Grass, but my job is to convince the interests which are to be involved, from sporting bodies through middle-ground conservationists to Societies for the Protection or Prevention of This and That, who inevitably include –'

'Antis,' Keith said.

'– that they can form a useful partnership. I've got to get

them to nominate suitable and open-minded persons to the board. And they've got to agree to Mr Grass's final stipulation – that the first project to be run under the new banner is to be a comparison between the estate and another of similar size which has been unshot for most of this century. There is to be a count of bird species and populations, and it is obligatory that the results are published. Is the idea as provocative as I think it is?'

'At first glance,' Keith said, 'yes. But it can be counted on to start the new body off without any misconceptions about the balance of nature taking over where shooting leaves off. All right, I'll expect you to pick me up on Monday. And Molly.'

THIRTEEN

Over the weekend the sun decided that it had poured out enough unaccustomed warmth over Scotland. High cloud drew shadow over the land. People resumed the vests and cardigans which they thought they had put away until Autumn. 'Back to normal,' became a usual greeting.

Keith had crammed a fortnight's work into a few days and he was glad to collapse into the luxurious grip of the Rolls. Somehow Molly had seemed to perpetually at his elbow and yet never quite available for a chat. Now, seated cosily between the two men, she chattered nonstop to the solicitor without seeming to ignore her husband. The two men sank into stunned silence.

There was drizzle over the high centre of Scotland, but they descended at last into a calm, close, misty day that held the west in a moist cocoon.

Mr Enterkin, without any great enthusiasm, suggested that they might join him for lunch at the inn; but Molly stated flatly that she had telephoned Whinkirk House and committed herself and Keith to lunching there. The solicitor quitted the car, singing to himself, while they drove on to Whinkirk House. Keith discovered, without surprise, that Molly had also bespoken separate rooms.

They ate a good but silent lunch, under the eye of Mr Roach. The idea was dawning on Keith that he must have done something wrong, although he could not for the life of him think what it could be. He decided that she would probably tell him in her own good time. 'I've got to go out,' he said.

'To the inn?'

'No. Ralph Enterkin's coming over here later. Do you fancy a dander in the country, or is the weight getting to be too much for you?'

Molly said that she thought she's stay and find her way around the house and garden.

Mr Enterkin's lunch, although plainer and served later, was also more cheerful than Keith's. He had to wait until the bar closed before Penny Laing was free to join him in the dining room. They sat down together. Penny was in great form. Since the demise of her husband under a runaway tractor some six years before, she had rarely had the pleasure of eating a meal that she had not herself cooked. To have a paid-for meal, as slap-up as the inn could provide, in the company of her lover and served by her boss at his most paternal made the meal into a great occasion for her.

'Did you have the car in London with you?' she asked.

Mr Enterkin, pending the disposal of a large mouthful of chop with assorted veg, shook his head.

'It'd have done your image good with all the other lawyers,' she pointed out.

'You can't get the use of a car in London these days, and nobody gets out of the way for a Rolls any more. At home,' Mr Enterkin added, 'Keith walks around all the time with a shotgun, and *everybody* gets out of his way. Perhaps I should try that.'

'The Rolls didn't come back here.'

'Keith had it. I believe he turned up with it at a clay pigeon meeting yesterday and caused a sensation. Mark you, Hayes and the car should have been back here, but Hayes wanted to stay over and visit his sister.'

'Sister!' she said scornfully. 'Bert Hayes doesn't have any sister.' She waited in suppressed silence as Harvey Brown served wine. 'You shouldn't encourage him,' she said when they were alone again. 'He was in trouble with Mr Grass already for that.'

'Was he, though?'

'Yes indeed. Mr Grass was having a pink gin in the bar there one day, and in comes Mr Beavis. He owns most of the land west of here, 'though he's not often up from London. "Thought you were going to come and see me," he says, "next time you were in Town, and talk about this here old trust of yours," he says. And Mr Grass says, "But I haven't been in Town for a month or more." "But I saw your car there, day before yesterday," says Mr Beavis. "Which one?" says Mr Grass. "The Rolls, of course," says Mr Beavis, "or I wouldn't have noticed otherwise." And, to cut a long story short, it turns out that Bert Hayes had the car away, supposed to be back at the makers for something, I suppose the ashtrays were full, and you can guess the rest. Proper old row Mr Grass gave him, from what I heard.'

Mr Enterkin filed the information away in his mind for Keith's benefit. He had no objection to the investigation of the alleged murder, as long as the estate did not pay for it. 'Does the general give dinner parties?' he asked.

'Not very often.'

'Is he planning to have one soon?'

She raised her eyebrows. 'Why, how would I know that?'

'I'm prepared to bet that you do. You are omniscient. Try.'

She thought for a few moments. 'Well, when he does, his daughter usually goes over to prepare it for him. And she usually asks Mrs Brown to go over and sit with her children. Not always, mind you, but usually. And when she does, Mrs

119

Brown warns me to take over the kitchen here. And she hasn't.'

'So,' said Mr Enterkin, 'it doesn't sound likely that he's planning a dinner. But Keith says that Brutus pinched a big pheasant out of his kitchen.'

'That's a useful little dog to have.'

'Keith gave it back. He had to, the general had seen him. Of course, pheasants are about as far out of season as they can get. The general explained that it had been frozen, and he was going to give a dinner party. Well, you *can* freeze a bird in full feather, but it isn't usual, and Keith said that it didn't feel as if it had been frozen, he said it felt limp and slightly warm. And the kitchen door was open, and Keith saw two or three more of them on the table, all cock birds.'

She met his eyes. 'I think you'd have to talk to Mr Winter about that sort of thing,' she said, 'not to me.'

Mr Enterkin struggled to his feet. 'Will you excuse me for a minute?' he asked. 'I think I'll make a phone call.'

There was still much of the estate which Keith had yet to walk over. He decided to kill two birds with the minimum of shot by walking to North Farm.

The sun was still in hiding but the mist had cleared. Keith was happy to be out in the open again, and with the familiar weight and balance of his own gun hooked over his arm. Brutus was quivering with pleasure. He romped for a few minutes and then settled down into hunting a zigzag pattern in front of Keith, well within gunshot.

The route was easy to follow. After half a mile, they encountered Winter, removing a dead rat from a Fenn trap set in a tunnel beneath the corner of a hedge. Winter seemed glad to straighten his back and chat for a few minutes about the unwelcome build-up of the pigeon population. 'The farmers want every gun out. The last thing I could thole would be a lot of shooting, just at this time; but if I refuse, the farmers'll blame me for every bittie of crop damage and I'll not get the help I need.'

'You can't win,' Keith said sympathetically. 'And did you know that you're being poached? Somebody's been setting dunce's caps.' He described the location of the small spinney.

Winter took out a cigarette. 'I can't pretend to be surprised,' he said at last.

'You know who's doing it, don't you?'

'Do you?'

'Not to be sure,' Keith said. 'But there were some cock-pheasants in a certain kitchen, and one of them had a stickiness about its head. The gentleman concerned says that they'd been frozen and he was thawing them out for a dinner party, but it doesn't seem likely at this time of the year, and I'm told that there doesn't seem to have been any dinner party either.'

'You're speaking about the general?'

Keith nodded.

'Well, it's a relief to talk about it,' Winter said with a small sigh. 'I'd been wondering if Mr Grass would've wanted me to tell you. You're nae here for long, and you've enough to do — time enough, I thought, when the new director's appointed. Tell the truth, I just wasnae sure *what* to do. I've kent about the general for years, and I told Mr Grass. The general was poaching awa', saving up unplucked pheasants in that freezer of his, and then thawing them out and selling them to the hotels at the very start of the season when prices were high.

' "Damn the man," says Mr Grass, "but at least he's sticking to cocks after they've served their turn". Then, last winter, I'd to speak to Mr Grass again. "Getting to be too much of a

121

good thing, isn't it?" he says. "I wish he'd stick to snaring a few bunnies. Leave it to me, Winter," he says, "and I'll speak to him".'

'And did he?'

'I dinnae ken. He died soon after.'

Keith was troubled. He held the general in the sort of affection that a man has for an unruly pet dog. 'It's all very well saying that the cocks have done their job, but they're a harvestable asset belonging to the estate and part of next year's shooting. It's not for us to be generous. Whatever Mr Grass's attitude may have been during his lifetime, his will reads differently. I suppose I'll have to have a word with the general.'

'Make it a firm one,' Winter said. 'Dinnae go soft wi' the blighter. He may be gey old, but he's as fit as a flea. Mr Grass would say, "He canna' hae muckle siller, an' he needs an interest in life", but if you ask me it's plain bloody thieving.'

'He sees himself as John Macnab, but we see him as Bill Sykes,' Keith said sadly.

'That's as maybe. How's your dog coming?' Winter seemed relieved to turn the subject. The buck had been firmly passed.

Keith looked down at Brutus who was lying relaxed at his feet, and the young dog looked up, conscious of being the subject of interest, and thumped his tail twice. 'He's coming along very well,' Keith said. 'Steady as a rock, and retrieving fur and feather already.'

'Now's your chance to show me,' Winter said. 'Pigeon coming over.'

Keith closed his gun. Sure enough, a fat pigeon was following the line of the hedge, drawn to join the flock feeding in a distant field. Keith raised his gun. As he swung through, the bird passed the trunk of a tree and Keith's gun checked its swing. He missed behind. The pigeon swerved and accelerated away, drawing with it like a shadow Brutus, who was straining every sinew to stay vertically below the bird and catch it when it dropped. Soon he was out of sight.

Winter forced the smile off his face. 'Well, he's keen,' he said.

Brutus was well aware of having broken the first rule of his training, and he was in no hurry to return and face the music. By the time that he had come back, suitably chastened, to heel, an hour had gone by. Keith, infuriated by the bad behaviour and by the knowledge that to punish a dog on its return was a fundamental error in training, would have given up and gone back to Whinkirk House to await Mr Enterkin. But a good trainer stops on a victory, never on a defeat. So he pressed on towards North Farm, keeping Brutus strictly to heel (which he hated), and was rewarded by dropping three pigeon with four shots and having Brutus perform to perfection.

The buildings of North Farm, when they came to them, were well kept and the yards were tidy and clean. They were guarded by quite the most ferocious dog that Keith had ever seen. It was, as Winter had said, half Collie; the other half seemed to have been mostly Alsatian with perhaps a trace of grizzly bear. Keith circled round well out of range, but Brutus trotted by with a display of nonchalance, just outside the stretch of the creature's chain and the reach of its teeth.

Mr Yates, whom they met a few yards further on, seemed deaf to the snarling of his beast, although Keith could hear him only with difficulty over the ominous noise. Yates was a man of about sixty, thin, tall and stooping, and bald but for a few random patches of hair that sprouted from his wrinkled scalp like ill-sown seed from ploughed land. His face wore a disagreeable expression of craftiness which turned out to be habitual, and his clothes were disreputable even for a working farmer, depending largely on binder-twine for support and cohesion.

Despite this unprepossessing appearance, Keith thought at first that he might have found a kindred spirit. The farmer was carrying a hammer-gun older than himself – by Playfair of Aberdeen, Keith noticed, and dating from perhaps 1870 – and a bag of the pigeon which he insisted were decimating his crops and garden and putting him in imminent danger of bankruptcy, and he was pleased to note, on comparing bags, that while Keith had made a small inroad into the problem his own was considerably larger.

'You've an interesting old gun there,' Keith said, 'but perhaps it's time you had a new one. If times are so hard, perhaps you'd like me to make you an offer?'

'Not for sale,' the farmer said, but he looked pleased. 'Belonged to my father. You'll no' find a harder-shooting gun around here. It got more cushies than your modern rubbish, didn't it?'

Keith's own Boss was thirty years old, and he suspected that the farmer had gathered his pigeon by spilling some tail-corn in the barn-yard and then shooting his birds on the ground from within the barn, but he knew better than to say so. He also knew better than to try to force a deal on price alone. 'Would you take ten quid to leave it to me in your will?'

'I'll think about it,' the old man said, but he was clearly tickled by the prospect of money in his hand in exchange for goods which he could retain for his lifetime. Keith for his part was quite prepared to spend twice the sum and wait a few years. Under the grime and some superficial rust, he could see a fine gun and the twist of the best pair of Damascus barrels that he had come across. They smiled on each other.

The bonhommie ended suddenly as the farm dog made a lunge and broke its chain near the collar. It hesitated for a moment, as surprised as any at its sudden release. Then it moved into a low, fast attack.

The two men froze, but Brutus kept his head. He would have rolled over in a possibly disarming gesture of submission, but the beast was coming not at him but at Keith, eyes and teeth gleaming white. And this was no ritual attack, to be broken off at the last instant.

Brutus gathered his strength and courage and went for the creature's throat. He got a firm but not a killing grip, and hung on for his life while the much bigger dog shook him around while seeking his own grip.

Keith was afraid to kick in case the jolt dislodged Brutus and gave the farm dog its chance. He dropped a cartridge into his gun, closed the breech and snapped off the safety catch.

The old farmer gave an inarticulate roar and hurled himself down on the two dogs, trying to tear them apart with his hands and nearly getting himself shot. A quick slash from his own dog set the first blood flowing.

Keith looked frantically around the yard. Outside what he took to be the milking-parlour there was a tap with a hose attached. Fumbling in desperate haste, he turned the water on, dragged the spluttering hose across and played it across the three scrambling figures. Brutus released his grip immediately and was as quickly gripped by the other dog. His screams shrilled around the yard. At close range, Keith blasted the hose into the big dog's mouth and nostrils. After a few seconds, reluctantly, it released its grip.

With a strength remarkable for his age, Yates dragged his dog to a shed, booted it inside and latched the door. He was sodden and blood from his hand and arm dripped over the cobbles.

Keith was down on his knees beside Brutus, holding his flesh together to minimise the loss of blood. Brutus was struggling to get on his feet. 'Use your phone,' Keith said. 'Call Whinkirk House for a car to take me to the nearest vet.'

Yates came back and picked up his gun. 'Don't you ever lift a gun to my dog,' he said.

'If he comes near my dog again, I'll blow him in half. Go and phone.'

'Aye. I will. You're no' welcome here. Give me back my letter of permission.'

'The hell with you,' Keith said. 'How did Mr Grass's dog die? Was it like just now?'

The old man backed away. 'No,' he said. 'No, it wasna'.'

'Come up to Whinkirk House and see me about your tenancy,' Keith said. 'But if that bugger's still alive, don't bother coming.'

The furious barking of the big dog seemed to shake the buildings around the yard.

FOURTEEN

The first few days of a new era always remain clear and separate in the memory. Later, the days merge and only the major events stand out. When Keith was asked for his written statement, he found that he had reached that stage during that crucial week.

His days began to settle into a variable routine. While Molly relaxed, roaming with a camera or enjoying the sun in a deck-chair when it was fine, or spending duller weather in front of a log fire, Keith busied himself about the estate's business. Whenever he could, he walked with his gun, and Brutus was always with him. Brutus knew, as dogs know these things, that Keith was in his debt, and he took to walking on Keith's right so that the shaved area and the sixteen stitches around his left shoulder were in clear view.

But, reluctantly, Keith had to spend much of his time in the house, dealing with the setting-up of the trust and seeing, on Mr Enterkin's behalf, most of the callers to the house. For Mr Enterkin seemed to be unaccountably busy at the inn.

First came the general, early in the day, vast and breezy as usual. 'Wanted to see me? Got message. Walked over. Nothing wrong about lease?'

'Not your lease,' Keith said. 'It's about the shooting. The executors have been spelling out the conditions.'

'White coat when I shoot,' the general said. 'Understood.'

'Not quite. If you want to retain the shooting privileges, you must wear the white coat whenever you're after any kind of game or vermin whatever. That means that you will lose those privileges if you are found on the estate without your white coat but with any means whatever of taking or catching any live creature.' Keith was looking the general full in the eye. 'And that includes any kind of gun or catapult, longbow or crossbow, airgun, traps, snares, treacle, raisins, sulphur or jam-jars. It also includes being accompanied by any dog which appears to have a trace of greyhound or whippet in its ancestry. You may carry spirits on your person, provided that you are not at the same time carrying any kind of nuts, fruit or other feed attractive to wildlife.'

The general sat and stared at him, his moon-face getting redder and redder. 'Finished?' he barked.

Keith thought swiftly. 'Fish-hooks,' he said. 'They're out too. I'll notify you of anything else as I think of it.'

But Winter, when Keith told him of the interview, was pessimistic. 'It'll maybe stop him for a week or two,' he said. 'But old habits die hard, and the general needs some excitement in his life. After he's got used to the idea that we ken a' about him, it'll just add to the thrill of having something at stake. He thinks his fieldcraft's so good that nobody'll ever catch him.'

'If he does,' Keith said, 'he'll come empty-handed a few times first. Try creeping up behind him and saying "Good morning, general." '

'M'hm. But,' Winter said, 'suppose he takes to a torch and an airgun? A white coat'll not show up muckle on a black night.'

When Roach announced Mr Yates, Keith braced himself for another confrontation, but instead of the old farmer a neatly dressed man in his middle thirties walked in. He had an open and honest face and a shock of sandy hair, and he shook hands like a man.

'I was sorry to hear about the argie-bargie you had with my dad the other day,' he said as soon as he was seated. 'He's ageing and not always wise. He's almost retired now. I do all the work and run the place.'

Keith had heard that sort of claim from sons before. 'It seems well kept,' he said politely.

Young Mr Yates smiled his frank and open smile. 'Mr Grass aye kept his tenants up to scratch,' he said. 'How's your wee dog?'

'Recovering.'

'I'm glad of that. He's coming along well, from what I hear.'

'Which is more than can be said for yon savage bugger you keep,' Keith pointed out.

Yates made a pretence at clutching his chest. 'Right between the third and fourth ribs,' he said. 'But don't put the blame on me, that beast's the apple of my dad's eye and he'll never part with it. I'd be shot of it in a minute if I could – it puts the shits up me – but I've got to own it's a grand watchdog. Surprisingly good at sheep, too.'

'At eating them?'

'At working them, as long as it's watched. Unless it's working, it's on that chain. And Dad's bought a new chain that'd hold a battleship in a gale.'

'And he sent you to get me to change my mind?'

'Something like that.'

'I heard,' Keith said slowly, 'that it was off its chain the night Mr Grass's dog died.'

'That's absolutely untrue.' Yates' eyes were so level and honest that Keith was sure that he was lying.

'Who shot the dog?'

'My father.'

'You saw it happen?'

Yates paused and then shook his head. 'My father's the tenant . . . on paper,' he said. 'But he's an awkward old bugger to deal with.'

'I never doubted it,' Keith said. 'He can take the dog with him when he goes.'

Yates leaned forward and cleared his throat. Suddenly his smile was tainted by guile, and he reminded Keith irresistibly of the old man. 'If you're terminating the old tenancy, why don't you make out a new one in my name? You'd find me much easier to deal with. You know fine the difference a co-operative farmer can make to the shooting.'

'Have you enough capital to stock the place?'

'I'd have my father's stock. He'd need to let me have it, or we'd both be out on our ears.'

'He might sell it and retire.'

'When he dies —'

'That's something I'm not prepared to discuss before the event.'

'If you wait for the event,' Yates said, 'you'll be too late. We'll be gone.'

Keith thought it over. He found that his wrath had been cooling as fast as Brutus healed. 'Against my better judgment,' he said, 'your father won't get a notice to quit just now. But just let me hear of one more incident involving that bloody dog . . .'

'You won't,' Yates said grimly. 'It just might be that that dog'll be the next to meet with an accident.'

'Purely as a matter of interest, what sort of gun do you use?'

'I share the old man's gun. By the bye, he says that for a consideration of twenty-five quid he'll will it to you. But it's time I had one of my own. Could you put me in the way of picking up a good used gun?'

'I suppose so,' Keith said. 'What could you go to?'

'I want something good,' Yates said. 'I've got some money that the old man doesn't know about. But I'll have to knock a nothing off the end when I tell him what I paid, so don't you go and clype on me. Well, shall I tell him it's a deal? Will you draw up the necessary agreement?'

Keith paused again for thought. He visualised the perfect twist of those barrels, browned and polished. It would be a collector's item. 'I suppose so,' he said.

Another visitor was a Mrs Ambrose. She made an appointment and arrived on time, a woman fighting a battle of compromise with the years. Her clothes were delicate and feminine without being too young for her, and she rustled as she walked. Her hair was beautifully done, tinted back to what Keith thought was probably the original colour and then intriguingly streaked with silver. Her eyes were still beautiful, made larger by clever making-up. When she shook hands, her hand in his felt naked through her glove. Keith, who had a certain expertise in such matters, put her down as a very dangerous lady.

She accepted coffee and insisted on pouring for both of them. Her accent resembled Alice Wyper's, but Keith judged that she had learned it later in life.

'The solicitor wrote to me about the silver, but when I rang up I was told that you were the person to speak to.'

'There was no need for you to come trailing away here, though,' Keith said. He was just making conversation while he enjoyed her legs. She had enchanting legs, and she was not secretive about them. And Molly was remaining celibate. 'I could have brought it to you and we could have discussed anything else at the same time.'

She smiled sweetly. 'It was no trouble. And I wanted to see

131

the place once more, just as Ray knew it, before it's all changed.'

Keith looked down at Mr Enterkin's notes. 'Mr Grass left you all his silver cutlery and a number of items of antique silverware, to quite a substantial value. It's all boxed now, but I have a list here.'

She waved it away. 'I'm sure it'll be all right.'

'So am I. But please check it carefully against the list when you unpack it. I'll have Hayes bring the boxes to you. Does he know where to come?'

'I think so,' she said. 'But Ray usually walked over, and the name isn't on the gate, so he may not. Tell him the house with the yellow paintwork.'

Keith heard his spoon rattle in the saucer. So this was the lady from whose doorstep, according to Winter, the dog had strayed. The story seemed more believable, with this lady attached. He dragged his mind back to business. 'As Mr Enterkin's letter mentioned, there's also a legacy of money.'

'But with a condition, he said.'

'Yes. Nothing very onerous. You are to attend the service —'

'In some outrageous costume, or lack of it?' She sounded mildly amused and nothing more.

'I think you'll feel adequately clad,' Keith said. 'You're to come dressed as a black sheep — the costume will be provided — and to sing *The Lord is my Shepherd*. To Brother James' Air. Unaccompanied.'

For the first time, she seemed shaken. 'I can't sing,' she said.

'I don't really believe that,' Keith said. 'You have a very musical voice.'

'When I try to sing, I sound *exactly* like a sheep.'

'Perhaps that's why you were chosen,' Keith said. He

fought to keep a straight face. 'I'm sure that your best attempt will be acceptable.'

'It'll just have to do,' she said sadly. 'I'm afraid Ray was always inclined to let his sense of the ridiculous run away with him.'

Mr Enterkin's advice had been to mention the condition and then to get off the subject as quickly as possible. 'Mr Grass must have had a high regard for you,' Keith said. 'His death will have come as a terrible shock.'

'Quite terrible,' she agreed. 'I was expecting him for a drink that evening, you know, but he never arrived. I . . . preferred not to telephone. To be honest, I thought he'd probably met up with some little tramp. I'm afraid Ray was always a lad for the girls, and being a bachelor he'd no need to change his ways as the years went by. As a matter of fact, I think he was getting worse,' she added dispassionately. 'He exercised a sort of *droit de seigneur* over his tenantry, and he owned most of the houses for miles around. So when he didn't turn up I just naturally assumed that one of the cottagers' daughters had had her sixteenth birthday. I mean, whatever people said about him he did usually wait for the age of consent. And then, in the morning, there was the news that he'd been found dead, and some people were hinting that he'd been murdered, and others were saying that it wasn't his body at all but that he'd done something silly and gone into hiding.'

'What did you think, yourself?' Keith asked. He shifted his position slightly and gained another inch.

'I could believe that he'd been murdered. I could believe that easier then I could believe in an accident, because Ray was always very careful with his skin. But he'd never have gone off without letting me know. In fact, if he'd wanted to go into hiding I'd have hidden him. He knew that.'

133

'But you're not, are you?'

She gave what was meant to be a musical laugh. It did sound rather like the bleating of a lamb. 'If I were,' she said, 'I'd hardly tell you.'

'I suppose not.'

'It's difficult to believe that he's dead, though,' she said. Obligingly, she crossed her knees and turned slightly. 'He was always so vital and alive. All my life he's been here, and now he isn't any more. My husband liked him too. Jim was very upset at the news.'

'Jim's your husband?' Keith had assumed her to be a widow.

'Yes. Which reminds me. Ray always said that he'd leave Jimmy his big telescope, the one on the tripod.'

'It's left to you. You'll find it with the silver.'

'Jimmy will be pleased. You see, he's been in a wheelchair for years. That's why he liked me to have other friends. And Ray never having married . . . You know, Mr Calder, if I hadn't married Jimmy, Ray would probably have asked me to marry him.'

'Perhaps that's why he stayed single,' Keith suggested tactfully.

'Do you think so?' She seemed pleased. 'Well, we'll never know now. You must come up and see us one of these evenings, Mr Calder.'

Keith rang the bell for Bessie to come and show Mrs Ambrose out. He himself could not have walked without embarrassment.

FIFTEEN

The day-to-day management of the estate, the need to plan for the future and tactical moves in preparation for the imminent first meeting of the new board necessitated daily contact between Keith and Colin Winter. A tacit competition arose between them as to which would visit the other on his home ground, because while Winter had come to appreciate the excellent coffee that was served at Whinkirk House, Keith had come to enjoy Mrs Winter's scones.

They sat on the Thursday morning in what would always be known as Mr Grass's study. Winter had been quicker off the mark, using the round of his traps as an excuse for being unavailable at home. The table was littered with maps and graphs and typescript.

'Is more land really needed?' Keith asked. 'The estate's a fine size the way it is. I know Mr Grass's will made provision for buying in Wellhead Farm, but that doesn't mean that we've got to take it over.'

'I've been thinking,' Winter said, 'and it's needed. The present estate's developed as far as it'll go. If we're to do what yon trust papers say, and to do teaching and research into the making of habitat, we've no spare land to do it on without spoiling what we've already got. But yon Wellhead's no' a bad wee parcel of land. You can see it from the window here.'

'Where the ground rises beyond the loch? It's got no cover on it.'

'That's my very point,' Winter said. 'We'd be free to

demonstrate the planting of cover, and since it wouldnae be part of the real shoot we could tear it apart and do it again. And it could still be farmed to earn its keep.'

'If you want me to support you when the board meets you'll have to convince me first, and you'll have a job. It's a Mr Benton, isn't it?'

'Mrs Benton. Her man died four or five years back.'

'Owner or tenant?'

'Owner.'

'I'd better go and take a look at it. Like to come with me?'

'I'll do that. But we'd better no' carry guns. She's let the shooting to a small syndicate.'

'All right,' Keith said. 'No guns. Shall we go now?'

They set off a few minutes later. Brutus came along, but he made it clear that he thought the men improperly dressed without their shotguns.

They took their time along the way, looked at nests, counted coveys, searched for traces of stoats or weasels, swept the skies for crows. Climbing a gate in a hedge, they disturbed a large, ginger cat feeding on the remains of a pheasant poult. The cat fled with Brutus in full cry behind, leaving its prey on the grass. 'Isn't it just damnable,' Winter said disgustedly, 'the things you see when you're no' carrying a gun.'

Keith grunted agreement. Bessie the maid had been giving him come-on signals.

As they threaded their way past the loch, keeping outside its immediate cover, Winter said, 'We winna' ging near the bank.' But even from a distance, Keith could see and admire. The loch was a natural feature but had been sculpted, with infinite labour, to provide a fretwork of bays and small islands, all carefully planted, giving dozens of nesting-sites and loafing-places. Brood after brood of Mallard ducklings were on show. Where a small creek served a boat-house they had a closer view of the water and Keith could make out a number of small waders. And then it was shut off by trees. They passed a strip of kale and began a climb through pasture to an unbroken fence beyond.

'This is the boundary,' Winter said.

A long strip of Jerusalem artichokes lay beyond the fence. 'She seems to go in for game crops too,' Keith said.

Winter snorted. 'Dinnae you be fooled,' he said. 'It's just at the march, to attract our birds so's they can drive them on into her land. She feeds a couple of wee ponds too, and our duck flight to and fro. She just got the idea a year or two back. Now she steals a lot of our birds, and takes a few hundred for the shooting. The bugger,' Winter added.

'A bad neighbour policy.'

'You're right. Fair greedy.'

Beyond the artichokes, the ground continued to rise. There were a few small fields of roots, but most of the land was given over to pasture. 'All the same,' Keith said, 'she's got some good beasts.'

'They're no' hers. She just lets the grazing.'

Keith looked around at the fences and up at the buildings. 'It needs money spent,' he said.

'It's costing us money. Those birds are a cash crop.' A noisy tractor was approaching, following a track across the face of the hill. 'This is herself,' Winter said. 'She was one of the Cunninghams from over the other side, the moneyed folk. But her and her brother were aye the black sheep. They cut her off when she married, and gave her the farm to get shot of her. It was smaller then, the Bentons have added more land. You'll find her a tartar.'

Winter's prediction was accurate. She stopped the tractor abreast of them and looked down from its seat as if from horseback, or from the howdah of an elephant. She was a woman in her forties with a voice so piercing that she had no need to stop her engine, while Keith had to shout to make himself heard. She looked ill, Keith thought. A shotgun of good quality was clipped under the seat, and a fox and two rabbits swung behind. Throughout their discussion she ignored Winter as though he had been invisible.

'You're Calder, aren't you? You're helping the lawyer who's handling Ray Grass's estate. Not left me anything, has he?'

'I'm afraid not.'

'Never thought that he would. I was never one of his women. He tried to add me to his collection, but I wasn't having any.'

She had been good-looking once, in a hard, classical mould, but was tired and faded now with lines of suffering eating into her face. If the late Mr Grass had ever turned his attention to her, Keith thought, it must have been some years before. She looked spent. Only her piercing voice still rang with the hauteur which she must have had in her youth. Keith tried, and failed, to find a suitable formula for reply, one which would acknowledge her virtue without denigrating her charms.

'Well, what did you come here for? Going to make me an offer?'

She was a little too eager. Keith, who had just decided to make a tentative start to negotiations, changed his mind. Let her worry for a while. 'Mainly a social call,' he shouted. 'Neighbours. And to see whether my manly charms might not persuade you to stop feeding the boundary, or to do your share of the rearing.'

'I'm within my rights,' she snapped.

'Legally, perhaps. But morally you know you're wrong.

Unethical. You plant an attractive crop just over the boundary from a neighbour who sweats blood to keep up a wild population and tops it up with releases. You sit here, doing no other work and not spending a ha'penny, and on shooting mornings you drive them inwards. Not neighbourly.'

'It's tough at the top,' she said bitterly. She pointed towards Whinkirk House. 'It was easy for him. With all that money, he could afford to waste land. But I don't call that efficient farming.'

Keith followed the direction of her eyes to the intensive cropping of the fields below, and contrasted it with the grazing above. He tried not to raise his eyebrows. 'Man isn't the only animal on earth you know,' he said. 'We have to make some provision for the others.'

'Just to shoot them?'

'Taking a chance over the guns is the rent they pay. It seems a small enough price to me.'

'Being shot?' She glared at him, almost savagely. 'That's too high a price to pay for anything. I'd rather be dead.'

Keith was to remember later that he had hidden a smile at the apparent contradiction in those last words. 'You let your shooting,' he said.

'You may not know it, young man, but there's such a thing as economic necessity. And if Ray Grass's manly charms couldn't persuade me, yours certainly won't. You'd better save them for your barmaid.'

Her words nearly started a train of thought at the back of Keith's mind. But the effort of arguing at the top of his voice was telling on him and he could feel his temper beginning to slip. 'Perhaps I will,' he said. 'Instead of persuasion, perhaps I should be looking for the big stick.'

Keith's words had been spoken at random while he

searched for more cogent arguments, and he was surprised to see her flinch. It occurred to him for the first time that she might be vulnerable to economic or other pressure.

When she spoke again her voice, although still lofty, was more reasonable. 'I've been thinking of starting a stable and riding-school,' she said. 'I'd have no objection to selling the land and keeping the buildings. You wouldn't find me hard to deal with.' And after a pause, she went on again, grudgingly. 'Sorry I spoke like that. I'm not very well.'

'How much were you thinking of asking?'

She named a figure which startled him. It was less than the maximum provided in Mr Grass's will, but still a great deal of money.

'How many acres?'

'Nearly a thousand.'

'Eight hundred and forty,' Winter said, almost into Keith's ear.

Keith forced himself to smile. 'That's almost twice the market value,' he shouted.

'Come off it,' she said. 'What if it is? Ray provided at least that much in his will.'

'And if he did, the estate isn't obliged to spend that much.'

She blazed up, and for a moment he could see the termagant that she must have been in her youth. 'Very well,' she said grimly. 'But you'll be sorry if I sell the land to somebody with sporting aspirations but short of spare cash. Being next door to a major sporting estate never did values any harm. They'll sit here for ever, milking you of your bloody birds.'

'Maybe. I'll think it over. Time's on my side. You'll not get that price from anyone else, and if the estate has to pay that much I don't care whether it's paid to you or to whoever follows you. If you drop the price, let me know.'

'I'd rather . . .' She broke off, and started again in a more conciliatory tone. 'I'd rather settle the matter soon. I want to get ahead with the stables.'

'It's tough at the top,' Keith said, and turned away.

As they started back down towards the sunlit loch they heard the tractor move off with a jerk behind them. Brutus, who had kept his distance from the noise and angry voices, fell in beside them.

'She's nae pleased,' Winter said. He sounded amused.

'She doesn't have to be pleased,' Keith said grumpily. 'Anyway,' he said, 'I'm glad she's doing something about the foxes.'

'She sells the furs,' Winter said, 'not that they fetch much more than the price of a cartridge at this time of year. If she'd any sense she'd have left it until it had its winter coat, but she's that desperate for money she'd be feared somebody else'd get it first. God, but she's looking her age these days,' he added, 'and I never realised what big feet she had until I saw her up on the tractor.'

Keith's throat was still sore from all the shouting. They walked in silence as far as the loch. Then he asked, 'Does everyone around here shoot?'

'Just about,' Winter said. 'Wi' the right sort of friends or the right sort of job, you shoot game. If not, you stick to pigeon and rabbits, or go down to the Firth after geese and ducks on the foreshore. And some come out as beaters and pickers, and get on the keepers' shoots at the tail-end.'

'And how many use home-loaded cartridges?'

'The most of them, at least for game-loads. I've aye loaded my own. Some of the men in the village share a machine between them. And the rest just buy their cartridges off them or off me. The farmers usually get from me in exchange for grain for the birds.'

141

'And you all use Joe Merson's shot?'

'Oh aye,' Winter said. 'I don't want the beggar about the land again, but I wish he'd come back just long enough to pour some more. Or I'll have to be buying the real stuff again. Man, that's a terrible price.'

SIXTEEN

That day, Keith took his afternoon tea in Miss Wyper's office. While they discussed agenda items for the first meeting of the new board, Keith also laid out his materials and loaded the Roman Candle pistol for the general to fire his salute at the service, now only a few days off. Keith wanted the job done. He had a feeling that, after they returned to Newton Lauder at the weekend, they might not be coming back.

Molly had joined them, but not, apparently, to be sociable. She sat knitting in an aloof silence, just occasionally looking up at Keith with hurt eyes. Miss Wyper kept making nervous conversational overtures, trying without success to coax a response. Keith remained polite and considerate. Whatever was wrong, it must work itself out. Something told him that whatever he said would be wrong. He tried not to think back to the days of love and laughter.

The shrill sound of the telephone was a welcome interruption to as disjointed a discussion as Keith could remember. Alice Wyper took the call, listened for a moment and then covered the mouthpiece. 'It's Harry Bloom. From the inn. He says you know him.'

Keith thought back over the faces that he had met in the bar. 'Is he the chap with the half-inch forehead and knuckles trailing on the ground?'

Miss Wyper chuckled. 'That's the one,' she said.

'I liked him.' Keith took the handset from her. 'Calder.'

Harry's gruff voice sounded gruffer over the line. 'Mr Calder? We got a rabbit-shoot on this evening. A market-garden near here's being eaten out by the mappies. They've made a hell of a come-back there since the last mixy, and he's got permission from the farmer next door to shoot today, just the one day before the cattle go back in. Harvey said you might be on for it.'

'Hang on a moment,' Keith said. He looked at Miss Wyper. 'Want to go on a rabbit-shoot?' he asked.

She nodded violently.

'Harry, can Miss Wyper come along?'

'Is she safe?'

'Safe enough.'

There was a pause. 'We were hoping you could get Mr Grass's Range Rover.'

'You want the Range Rover, you get Miss Wyper as well.' He raised his eyebrows at Molly, but she shook her head. Keith should be safe with Miss Wyper and a gang of men. 'What time?' Keith asked.

'Come as soon as you can.'

Keith gave the telephone to Miss Wyper to hang up, and looked down at the Roman Candle – a wheel-lock pistol made in Germany some three hundred years before. He had probed for and counted the internal vents, and calculated that the pistol had been designed to fire up to thirteen shots from its four barrels. So far he had only inserted seven loads. But the fewer the safer. 'Put this by for the general,' he told Miss Wyper.

At about the time when the Range Rover was collecting a varied assortment of men, guns, dogs and nets from the inn, Mr Enterkin was stretching full-length on Penny Laing's sofa. She was on her knees, coaxing a log fire into life. She had a free evening, and there was tacit agreement that they would spend it in the proper savouring of food, wine and dalliance.

144

Mr Enterkin, looking fondly on her bent back, was suddenly siezed with an unlawyerlike impatience. 'I think,' he said, 'that it's time that we thought about getting married.'

Without looking round, she shook her head so that her hair danced. 'No,' she said, 'I'm not the wife for you. I'm all right for a cuddle and no harm done, but our lives are different. You're a solicitor from the other side of the country, and you'll go back there when this job's over. Just come and see me sometimes, at weekends. I'll be here as long as you want me.'

There was a silence. She poked at the fire. The flames lit a rosy halo round her head. 'The board will meet soon,' he said at last.

'You told me that.'

'One of the first items of business will be the appointment of a full-time director. They'll probably have a lot of grand ideas between them, and draw up a list of qualifications that'll only attract the kind of applicant we can't afford. And there may be some who'd rather see a glorified gamekeeper in the post. I've got to point out to them that what they really need is an organiser. Somebody who can take their policies, get advice, and put it all in effect. A degree in accountancy or the law would help. I thought that I might put in for the post myself.'

She turned round. 'You didn't! You wouldn't!'

'You don't know everything after all. I would.'

She pulled a cushion down onto the floor and knelt on it, laying her head on his chest. He began to fondle the nape of her neck. 'Bit of a come-down for you, wouldn't it be?'

'You have an exaggerated idea of the life-style of small solicitors. It's not an enormous salary, but free accommodation counts for a lot.'

'At Whinkirk House?'

'At Whinkirk House. I'd save a lot of money not having to travel all the way through here to see my –'

'Fancy woman?'

'– my lady-friend. If I did two conveyances a month and drew up the occasional will, I'd be rolling.'

She stirred under his hand. 'If it's what you want . . .'

'What I want is a wife.'

'Get one then, but not me. Can you see me up at the big house?'

'Easily.'

'The director's wife?'

'Why not?'

She sighed. 'I'll tell you why not. I'm just a barmaid, and a small farmer's widow. If I went up to the house it'd be to help with the cleaning.'

He gave her a pat on the back of the head. 'Now you just shut up and listen to me for a minute,' he said. 'I don't know what you think the director's wife would have to do, so I'll just tell you. She'd have to advise me about country things, because although I know about the law and accounts and how to organise things I must admit to a certain innocence about all things bucolic. You'd have to supervise the cooking and cleaning and housekeeping. You could do that, couldn't you?'

'Yes.'

'Serve drinks to visitors?'

She gave a muffled snort. 'Of course.'

'A lot of the visitors will be young keepers or agents who've never been far from home before nor stayed in a big house, and they'll be feeling a bit lost and alone. They'll need a nice, motherly soul –'

'Well,' she said, 'I like that!'

'– who'll make them feel at home.'

There was a silence but for the crackling of the logs. 'I thought,' she said at last, 'that you were supposed to do the kneeling down.'

'Let's keep things the way they are. Very suitable.'

'My knees are getting stiff.' They rearranged themselves, sitting close together on the couch. 'You don't want that job,' she said. 'You'd hate it. You just think I'd like it. Well, I'm not going to have you giving up your life and your friends just because I'm slow and stupid. You've told me what I'd have to do here. What would I have to do there?'

'In Newton Lauder, if you married me?' Mr Enterkin thought about it. 'Nothing very much. I live a quiet life. I don't give cocktail parties or go to big dinners. If I dine out, it's with friends like Keith. I don't bother to keep up with any Joneses. In fact, if you wanted to go on working as a barmaid, but in Newton Lauder, it wouldn't bother me one damn bit.'

'Your friend Keith Calder,' she said. 'He's the one you want for director.'

'I'd thought about it. I don't suppose he'd take it on, but I'll ask him. You like Keith and Molly, don't you?'

'They're all right.' Penny hesitated. 'I've only seen her the once, in the bar. She's a bit odd, isn't she?'

'You noticed? She isn't usually like that. She usually bubbles over with happiness. And she's devoted to Keith. I can't think what's come over her all week. It must be the baby. Well now,' Mr Enterkin said, turning back to more important matters, 'what about it?'

'I'll think it over.'

'But for how long?'

'I'll tell you,' she said,' . . . after we've had our dinner.'

The venue for the rabbit-shoot turned out to be much as Keith had visualised it – a small market-garden showing signs of serious rabbit-damage. Beyond the fences lay pastureland dotted with clumps of gorse. A small hillock bore a thick crest of the same gorse, and was scored by a thousand typical rabbit-scrapes and burrows.

Keith and Miss Wyper waited, as requested, in the Range Rover while the men, who were obviously accustomed to working as a team, set off on a flanking movement, walking very softly despite a load of assorted netting.

'Are they going to use ferrets?' Miss Wyper asked.

'Not at this time of year,' Keith said, shocked. 'Too many young in the buries, they'd have to wait a fortnight for the ferrets to come up to the surface again. By this time of a sunny day, there should be plenty of bunnies out and about. They'll use the long net around the jungly bit and purse-nets over the rest of the holes to back-net any rabbits that make it that far. The drill is, don't shoot any rabbits that're making for the nets. That way, youngsters and does in milk can be let go again.'

'That won't suit the market gardener, will it? And if it reduces the bag it won't suit me either.'

'Harry knows what he's doing. The vegetables were hopping with rabbits when we arrived, and he's put the young chap to cover the dead ground. They'll still be there. How many do you need?'

'I'm up to sixteen. But, if I go, I'll go decently clad. I want another ten. And,' she said, 'I'll get them, too. I went to a clay-pigeon school at the weekend.'

'And how do you feel about it all now?'

'In some ways, I can still hardly bring myself to do it. When you skin them, they're just like little people. And yet . . .'

'Yes?'

'I couldn't say I've formed my own opinions yet,' she said slowly. 'But I'm beginning to see the sense in what other

148

people have said. Mr Winter always told me that if pests have to be controlled you might just as well eat the meat. I can see that now. That's what we're here for, isn't it? And Mr Grass used to say that game-shooting was a branch of agriculture, you put them out, look after them and then harvest them. I suppose that's true in a way. But I can't feel quite comfortable about the natural species – wildfowl and so on. I mean, they're there, and we don't have any special right to predate on them.'

'Look at it this way,' Keith said with equal seriousness. 'They don't die in their beds as we do. Mostly, they die of cold or starvation, or get taken by a predator. Me, I'd as soon be shot. As long as man operates within the margin that'd die anyway in a hard winter, I don't believe that that species needs to be protected from him. But that's what the schedules to the Protection of Birds Act are all about.'

'I sort of see that. But it's not the way the . . . the other side see it.'

'Of course not. And maybe they're right. Maybe in a hundred years man'll have lost the instinct to hunt. Maybe not, we've had it a long time. I just happen to believe that it'll be a bad day for wildlife if it comes.'

'The general –' Miss Wyper stopped dead.

'What about him?'

'Oh, just that he invited me to go with him to a chicken-farm, one of those battery places, and see for myself whether that wasn't a crueller way to provide fowl for the table. I think I'll take him up on it. But I remembered something else. I was out early this morning, down towards the lake, and I saw the general slinking along. He didn't see me and he was trying not to be seen. I wondered whether it was something I should tell you or Mr Winter about.'

'Was he carrying a gun?' Keith asked.

'No. He had a fishing-bag over his shoulder.'

The general, Keith thought, would have been setting snares or otherwise continuing his poaching. 'I take it that he wasn't wearing a white coat?'

'Good Lord, no!'

'I'll have to have another very serious word with the old gowk,' Keith said uncomfortably. 'He just doesn't seem to take a telling. I suppose, on these dawn forays of yours, you've seen no sign of Joe Merson being back?'

'Harry Bloom's the person to speak to,' she said. 'He and Joe were often up to mischief together.'

They chatted on, desultorily. It was another half-hour before Harry Bloom stole quietly up to the Range Rover and put his head inside. 'Ready?' he asked.

Keith nodded. 'Have you seen Joe Merson lately?'

'Not for months. Now if you, Miss, would go and stand by that old shed, and for Pete's sake don't let them get underneath or we'll never get them out, and you, Keith, come and put your dog through the greens and we'll see what we get. Move quietly, mind. About old Joe, there's just the one thing fashes me.' Harry stopped and stared into the distance where a pair of lapwings were swooping and climbing over an empty field. 'I'd believe,' he said at last, 'that Joe'd just gone off, but for that one thing. He never went off, not of his own accord, without he'd bring his ferrets down for me to keep. And he didn't. Of course, he may've sold them.'

'Have you been up to his cottage to look?' Keith asked.

'Can't. Mr Grass caught me knocking his pheasants out of their roosts with a catapult in moonlight. He got an inderdict, stopping me coming onto the land for a year,' Harry said without resentment. 'But he gied me back the twenty quid I was fined. He was a gent, was Mr Grass.'

The frantic sport, the hurtling rabbits, the shots that

scored and shots that missed, none of these are any part of our story. It is of only slight relevance that Miss Wyper shot seven rabbits, and paunched them on the spot without turning more than a very few hairs. More pertinent, strange as it may seem, was the fact that one rabbit belonged to Brutus alone. The last rabbit of the day had avoided the guns and was streaking for an unguarded hole when Brutus overtook and grabbed it up. He took it straight to Harry Bloom, and by the time that Keith could get there was being praised and petted for what was in fact a gross breach of training. Keith threw up his eyes to the darkening heavens. He knew that months of patience would be needed to undo the damage and prevent the dog becoming a chronic runner-in.

Miss Wyper, who was becoming a favourite with the men, was invited to help with the delicate task of gathering up the nets, but Keith and the "young chap" were considered to be too ham-fisted. Keith smiled and went to sit on a wall and watch the sky change colour, and soon the boy came and sat near him. Brutus, who by now considered himself to be the only real expert present, was far too busy supervising the others to spare Keith a moment. Brutus' new-found pride and dedication were such that he would follow any man with a gun. Harry still had his gun with him, so he had a black shadow at his heel.

'Mr Calder, may I talk to you for a moment?' The boy was well-spoken. His voice reminded Keith of somebody.

'Yes, of course.'

'We weren't properly introduced. I'm Bob Ambrose.'

'Ambrose. Didn't I meet your mother a few days ago?'

'Yes. That's what I wanted to talk to you about. You've got something to do with Mr Grass's will, haven't you?'

'Not a lot, but something. I'm dogsbodying for the

executor. I'll help you if I can without cutting across anybody else's right to confidentiality.'

Bob Ambrose looked round. The others were well out of earshot, but he lowered his voice all the same. 'You know about the situation at my home?'

'I know that your father's been in a wheelchair for some years,' Keith said.

'Is he my father?' the boy asked, barely above a whisper. 'Or was Mr Grass? He left my mother a legacy . . .'

Keith took a few seconds for mental adjustment. Neither by nature nor by upbringing had he ever had strong feeling about legitimacy; and only with his own marriage had he gained, and at second hand, any feeling for the sanctity of that institution. Only the imminence of a son or even – a staggering thought – a daughter of his own had caused him to start rethinking his attitudes. But young Ambrose, brought up amid ethical conflict, had drawn his own conclusions and was desperate for reassurance.

'I don't think,' Keith said, 'that you were one of his bequests. In fact, we can be sure of it. He did, as you know, leave behind a number of bairns born on the wrong side of the blanket. Since he never married, he could hardly have left any other kind. But in every case he left a bequest to the child, not to the mother. Those bequests are absolutely confidential, but I can tell you that you're not included.' Privately, Keith thought that it took a wise man to know his own children, and he could not even be sure of counting himself among their number.

The assurance satisfied Bob Ambrose. He relaxed visibly. 'Thank God for that!' he said. 'You can't know . . .'

'How old are you? Sixteen?'

'Seventeen.'

'Your father's accident?'

'Polio, when I was three. It's not that. But Ray Grass was a close friend of my mother's from long before that. I know exactly what he was, and what my mother is.' He turned his face away from Keith. He might have been watching a distant flock of rooks squabbling their way to roost. 'It's not that I've anything much against bastardy. But there were those two. And then there's Dad. I wanted one decent, honest person in my pedigree.'

'Try to believe the best,' Keith said gently. 'Many women flirt around and pretend to be promiscuous who'd scream bloody murder if a man laid a finger on them. And, remember, she's played fair. It must have been hard for an attractive, red-blooded woman to find herself stuck with a crippled husband, but she's still around. She might have been forgiven if she'd run off with somebody else.'

'I wish she had,' Bob said. He sounded near to tears.

But on the journey home he recovered his spirits. He chatted away about the evening's doings, said a cheerful goodnight to the men who got out at the inn and was insistent that Keith and Miss Wyper come to his home for a visit.

'We couldn't bother your parents at this time of night,' Keith said.

The boy brushed this aside. 'My mother's bound to be out somewhere, and Dad does enjoy being visited at any time of the day or night. And he'll be needing a snack.'

The thought of a snack was persuasive, for they had missed dinner. Keith had to drop the boy anyway, and Miss Wyper, who had a room in the village, decided to come along and to walk back.

Inside the house with the yellow paintwork, Bob and Miss Wyper paid brief respects to Mr Ambrose and then disappeared in the direction of the kitchen, leaving Keith to chat with him.

153

'I won't shake hands,' Keith said. 'I've been gutting rabbits.'

Mr Ambrose smiled and forgave him. 'Sport was good, then?'

'Very. Your son's a good shot.'

'We'll have to see if we can't get him a better gun for his birthday.'

'Send him over to me,' Keith said. 'I'll fix him up.'

Mr Ambrose had been a big man, but his years in a wheel-chair had wasted his legs and overdeveloped his chest and arms. He seemed to live almost entirely in the one large room which had been equipped to suit his special needs. One end of the room was taken up by several large tables heaped with books and journals and charts and bound sets of accounts, a typewriter and some pages of manuscript.

'Are you the Ambrose who writes the articles and text-books about cost-effectiveness and current-cost accounting and all that jazz?'

Mr Ambrose laughed. His smile was so like his son's that Keith wondered why the boy had ever been worried about his own parentage. 'That sounds like me,' he said. 'I used to be an accountant, and I still do an audit now and again. But after I was stricken, I found that I had time to study the accounts of a whole range of firms, to separate the sheep from the goats and ask myself why one succeeds and another fails. It started as a hobby and grew from there.'

'It may be a hobby to you,' Keith said, 'but my partner used to be an accountant, and he quotes you as if you were the scriptures, usually when he wants to show me that some-thing I want to do wouldn't be good business. Could you give me a short course in How to Destroy an Accountant in Three Easy Questions?'

Ambrose laughed again. He was a happy man, despite his disability. 'Easily,' he said. 'I'll write them out for you, one of these days.'

A few minutes later, Keith broke off a general conversation. He looked down at his hands. 'I'd better wash before I eat,' he said. 'I'm told that humans can't get myxamatosis, but I'd rather play it safe.'

'There's one by the kitchen, and one at the head of the stairs.'

The house was large and rambling. Keith had expected to see lights or to hear noises which would lead him towards the kitchen, but the place seemed deserted. Rather than go back, he climbed the stairs and found a bathroom at the top. The corridor was as dark as the rest of the house. As he stood in the door, funbling for the bathroom switch, Keith saw a light shining under another door at the far end of the corridor. While he was looking, it flicked out. He tiptoed in that direction. There were tiny sounds from inside.

Keith hesitated. Mr Ambrose had mentioned that his wife was out, visiting an old school-friend, but Keith knew that a complaisant husband will often lie to save a reputation that is no longer worth saving.

On the other hand, Mrs Ambrose had said that she would have given Mr Grass asylum. And the boy had been very upset about her relationship with Grass.

Keith turned the handle gently and opened the door a few inches. A thickset figure was silhouetted against the drawn curtains. He put his hand to the wall, and before he even knew that he had found the switch the room was flooded with light.

Two figures stood by the window, so close together that they had looked like one. They were Mrs Ambrose and the younger Mr Yates, and a scrap of lace was the total of the clothing which they wore between them.

Before the two could react, Keith had switched off the light and closed the door. He tiptoed away. While washing his hands he also bathed his face and wrists in cold water.

Mr Ambrose, for all his confinement to a wheelchair, was an entertaining host. When Keith drew up the Range Rover at last outside Whinkirk House, the fields were dark and all was silence. The only light in the house seemed to be behind the front doors, which opened in response to the sound of his feet on the gravel. Against the yellow light stood a female figure. Keith's heart lifted at the thought of Molly. Then he saw that her hair was fair. Bessie the maid had waited up, to let him in and see to his needs.

SEVENTEEN

Keith was bolting a hasty breakfast next morning, trying to overtake Molly who was on her last sip of coffee, when Bessie came to the table. 'Telephone message from the inn, Mr Calder,' she said. 'Can you come over straight away? Mr Enterkin wants you.' Keith thought that she gave him the tiniest suggestion of a wink with the eye away from Molly, but whether this referred to the message or to something quite different, or was even a figment of his imagination, he neither knew nor cared. He looked at his watch.

'Tell him I'll be over in half an hour,' he said.

Five minutes later he gave Molly a polite kiss on the cheek, collected Brutus and his gun, and set off walking the now familiar tracks. The preceding fortnight spent walking the estate, at a time of year when he would usually have done his travelling by car, had restored him to his winter level of fitness, but today his pace was less then brisk and when a small flock of pigeon rose from beyond a hedge he yawned and walked on. Brutus glared at him.

At the inn, there was no immediate sign of Mr Enterkin. Keith begged a cup of coffee from Mrs Brown and took it out to a bench in the forecourt where he could lean the gun, in its sleeve, against the wall and sit quietly for a minute.

He had almost dozed off when he realised that a figure was standing over him, a tall, solid young man in a grey suit. He had a round, rosy face and brown curls, so that Keith's first impression was of a child's drawing sprung to life. Brutus, from under the table, decided that the newcomer's manner was properly respectful and that he must therefore be tolerated.

'Mr Calder? Harvey Brown said I'd find you out here. I'm Sergeant Yarrow. May I join you?'

'Please do,' Keith said.

The sergeant showed his warrant card. 'Strictly speaking,' he said, 'I'm C.I.D. But I've been detached for the moment to help Inspector Glynder with the matters you raised with him.'

'I see. He's taking it seriously, then?'

'Seriously, yes. Reluctantly, too, in view of the line he took at the fatal accident enquiry.' Keith got the impression that Sergeant Yarrow was amused but trying to hide it. 'He is finding other things to do just now. I'm to look into the matter and report back. For the moment, think of me as being in uniform. As soon as we're sure that we've got a criminal case, of course, it becomes the business of my proper department and I'm in plain clothes again.'

'I hope you're a bit of a quick-change artist, then,' Keith said. 'Because I don't think there's a damn bit of doubt about it. But go your own way. Do you want me to run over it again?'

'Please.'

'Do you shoot?'

'I've a gun,' the sergeant said. 'Just for the clay pigeons. But I load my own cartridges and a mate of mine pours shot, so I know the basics. That's partly why I was put on this job.'

'That's a help,' Keith said. Patiently, he took the sergeant through the ground that he had covered with Inspector Glynder. He kept his voice low for fear of eavesdroppers. The sergeant seemed to follow him very closely, taking brief notes and interrupting to ask an occasional question.

'That seems clear enough so far,' the sergeant said when Keith finished.

158

'What do you think, yourself?'

'I'm not here to think, I'm just gathering facts.'

Something in Sergeant Yarrow's voice reminded Keith of his initial briefing by Mr Enterkin. 'You gave evidence at the fatal accident enquiry, didn't you?' Keith asked.

'What if I did?' the sergeant asked sharply. 'That was just due to chance. I happened to be nearby, looking into a case of sheep-stealing, when the call came in that Mr Grass had been found shot. A car was sent with two uniformed lads, and I was told to look in just in case it was a criminal matter. Because I was nearer I got there first, so I was called to give evidence as the first officer on the scene. And that's all.'

'That's all,' Keith said, grinning, 'except that you had your own doubts. You started to voice them in court, and you were told to shut up. Right?'

'I don't think we need to –'

'What's more,' Keith said, 'you've been told to come here, go through the motions and make a negative report. Right?'

The sergeant said nothing. His face was impassive.

'In confidence,' Keith said, 'what didn't you like about it?'

Sergeant Yarrow looked round. The windows were closed and there was nobody near. 'In absolute confidence?' He lowered his voice almost to a whisper. 'The distances didn't look right. I measured them. If he was climbing the fence when he was shot, the maximum distance would have been the sixteen feet to where the gun ended up. And that's not to say that the gun hadn't done some of its sliding and bouncing after it went off. I gauged the barrels of the gun – I have my own gauge – and it was the old-fashioned game – boring, true cylinder on the right – and full choke on the left.'

Keith was frowning. 'I never saw the body,' he said. 'How big was the pattern-circle?'

'About six inches. It had smashed most of his face, but you

159

could make out the edge of the pattern clearly. Well, I reckoned that no full-choke pattern was going to open out that much inside sixteen feet. I've fired at a target at that sort of range, and as often as not the shot isn't even coming out of the shot-cup by then. Of course, now you tell me that that cartridge wouldn't have had a shot-cup anyway. I'd missed that point. I'm too used to clay-busting.'

'Even from a game cartridge,' Keith said, 'I'd expect a much smaller pattern than six inches. Could you get your hands on the gun again? We could run some tests.'

'I could try.'

'I'd like to have it for a few days, just to give it an overhaul to make up for some of the neglect it suffered in your colleagues' hands.'

'Sorry about that,' the sergeant said absently. 'Blast it! I'm pig-in-the-middle. You were right, I was told to come out and prove that there was nothing wrong, and in my mind I'm certain that there's been a murder done. If I go back and say so, without having any further proof, I'll . . .'

'You'll have your arse in a sling?'

'I wasn't going to put it just that way, but it expresses it admirably.'

'But if you were to go on investigating, and were to go back with proof positive, even an arrest . . .'

'I'd have to be on damn sure ground.' There was a silence while the sergeant glared at the table-top in front of them. Then he went on. 'You're right. All I can do is to gather it all up. I'll have to decide how to play the hand once I've got all I can get.'

'You could start by getting microphotographs, to prove that the extractor-marks on the cartridge which was in the gun were made by that gun,' Keith suggested.

'I can do that.' Sergeant Yarrow made a note. 'And I must

get samples of this poacher chap, Merson, the shot he pours. If that corresponds with the shot recovered from the late Mr Grass, at least we'll know that it was a local cartridge.'

'I don't want to worry you,' Keith said, 'but you're up against a number of snags. First of all, cartridges get passed from hand to hand. People borrow a few cartridges. Obviously they can't return the same ones. So reloads could turn up in the hands of somebody who always bought his cartridges off the shelf. Secondly, Merson hasn't been seen around since a few days after Mr Grass died. And, thirdly, Merson's shot probably never came out the same two days running. If he was using scrap lead, it could come from a dozen sources, wherever he could buy it or scrounge it or exchange it for finished shot. Sheet lead off a roof one week, an old bird-bath the next. Maybe battery-plates.'

'There still might be what you might call a chemical finger-print. My pal adds a little arsenical weedkiller, to increase surface tension. Then again, the shot seemed to be as hard as the shot that you buy. That suggests antimony, doesn't it?'

'That's right,' Keith said. 'And his easiest source of antimony would be printer's metal. And Enterkin said something about Mr Grass owning a print-shop somewhere.'

The sergeant was looking happier. He seemed relieved to have found a sympathetic ear on a helpful witness. 'I bow to your superior knowledge,' he said. 'I'd better go and look.'

'Shall we show you his cottage, or do you know where it is?'

'We?'

'The dog and me.'

'I never saw him under there. Isn't he well-behaved!' He scratched behind Brutus' ear.

'Would that it were ever so,' Keith said. Mr Enterkin's mode of speech sometimes rubbed off on him. 'We'd better walk. A car's a dead loss among the fields.'

'I found that out last time,' Sergeant Yarrow said.

'You don't mind if I carry my gun?'

'Shoot if you like, but don't shoot me,' the sergeant said frivolously.

Once out in open country Brutus got going again, questing to and fro in a satisfactory manner. The two men walked together, the sergeant tactfully dropping slightly behind.

'Do you mind if we talk?'

'Talk away,' Keith said. 'Miss Wyper — she was Mr Grass's secretary — she and I have been shooting over this ground for the last week or more, and the pigeon and rabbits aren't as trusting as they used to be. Everything else is out of season and knows it. So I'm not really expecting a shot, I'm just looking for the chance to do a little dog-training.'

'It's early to think of motives, but I was wondering whether you'd come across any.'

'Hundreds. Possibly thousands.'

'I thought he was well liked.'

'I believe he was,' Keith said, 'from what I hear. I met him once and I liked him, but that doesn't mean that I couldn't have had reason to want him dead. He was a bit of a joker and that got him a few enemies, although he usually made amends afterwards one way or the other. He seems to have been one hell of a man for the women, which is another way to get yourself misliked.' Keith was speaking from old and not altogether bitter experience. 'There may have been any number of husbands, fathers, brothers, boyfriends, grand-children, you name it, who'd have been just as happy to see him out of the way. But that's only the start of it.

'You also know, or if you don't I'm telling you, that to call him wealthy would be like saying that the Duchess of Argyll

162

was adequately provided for. Ralph Enterkin keeps trying to explain it to me, and whenever I think I've got the picture he points out that I don't know the half of it yet. Now, you can't get rich without making enemies, and when you *are* rich there's got to be somebody better off for your dying if it's only the taxman. About sixty individuals are mentioned in his will, a dozen or so charities and the local trust.'

'That's a lot of motives,' the sergeant said respectfully.

'I'm not finished. Mr Grass was a clever businessman and made a braw penny himself, but he got a head start from his father and his grandfather. Grand-dad Grass was an Englishman who made a packet out of agricultural machinery. Maybe they named grass after him, I wouldn't know. The point is, he settled up here and put his money into property. He didn't bother with rents and feuholds, he leased it out on ninety-nine year leases and used the money to buy more property. Most of those leases are almost up. In a large number of cases, Mr Grass's will permits the lessee to buy up the lease cheaply. But it's easy to be charitable from the grave. If he'd lived, he might not have been so generous.

'So you might find it easier to look for people who didn't have a motive. Murders, after all, have been committed before now just for a few pennies. Even you, yourself —'

'Oh, come on, now,' the sergeant said.

'I mean it. The police welfare fund comes in for a useful sum. The odds are that you'll benefit from that at some time or another. And the buildings occupied by your force are subject to one of the leases, which runs out in a couple of years. How do you fancy working out of some hastily converted attic?'

The sergeant treated the question as rhetorical and asked one of his own. 'Putting two and two together and coming up with a handful,' he said, 'can I take it that some of Mr Grass's famous conditions are attached?'

'You can. Any interference with the service next week, and the buildings are transferred to Civil Rights organisations and the welfare fund can whistle for its legacy.'

'Ah,' the sergeant said with satisfaction. 'That explains a certain atmosphere of frustration hanging like a cloud over my superiors. You don't seem to be doing much dog-training,' he added.

'I'm letting him learn for himself about scents and things.'

'Then why carry a gun? Not that I object, I'm just curious.'

'Because that black bastard,' Brutus acknowledged the description by a flick of his tail, 'doesn't bother, otherwise. He knows too damn well what –'

A rabbit bolted from under Brutus' nose. It was too much. He hurled himself after it, quite spoiling Keith's chance of a shot. Eventually and reluctantly he came back to the whistle, was scolded and put to heel, grumbling to himself. His experience the previous evening had proved, at least to his own satisfaction, that he could catch rabbits more effectively than Keith could shoot them.

'Ralph Enterkin wants to pass the hairy idiot on to me,' Keith said. 'He fancies getting himself some small pug whose idea of a walk will be much the same as his own. About ten yards. If I do take that beggar on, I swear I'll make a cheese-wire collar for him on the end of a long check-lead. The first time he runs in, he'll take his own stupid head off. The only certain cure.'

'That's the place up ahead, isn't it?' the sergeant said. 'I haven't approached it from this side before.'

At that moment it happened again. A rabbit fled almost from under their feet and Brutus took off like a greyhound. The rabbit outdistanced him easily along the path ahead of them. Where the path climbed the bank the rabbit bobbed to the right and dived into the brambles. Brutus crashed in in vain pursuit. Two hen pheasants squawked indignantly and whirred upwards while their chicks ran cheeping onto the grass.

Brutus came to his senses. It had been a lovely chase, but now the piper must be paid. He searched frantically for some placating gift. There was a familiar object under his nose. He snatched it up and turned back in answer to the approaching whistles.

Keith arrived, angry and half-winded. Brutus deposited his offering and shut his eyes against the wrath to come. Apart from a cuff across the ear that was almost a pat, the wrath never came. 'Take a look at this,' Keith said. 'A spent cartridge, and it's been reloaded in its time,'

'You think it might be the fatal one?' the sergeant asked, panting.

'Who knows. But there's a strict rule around here that you take your empties home with you. Did you see where he picked it up?'

'I couldn't see the ground. But he stopped and ducked his head somewhere near the base of that tall frond of cow parsley.' The sergeant paused and mopped his forehead. The breeze had dropped and the day was turning warm. 'You've had more experience of testing patterns,' he said. 'Suppose I go up to the fence and pretend to be Mr Grass.'

Keith nodded. The sergeant climbed the fence and then stood, with one foot on a lower strand of wire. 'Now,' he said. 'Come towards me until you think that a full-choke pattern would almost cover my face.'

'All right.' Keith opened his gun and showed the sergeant the empty chambers. He walked up the path and stopped. Against all his training, he raised his gun and sighted on the sergeant. He shook his head, walked another couple of paces and tried again. 'About here.'

165

'The gun definitely didn't slide that far. Now do it again for a true-cylinder barrel.'

Keith came forward three more steps. 'I'm guessing,' he said. 'But, with a plastic shot-cup, about here.'

'That's nearer where the gun fetched up. The cow parsley's just a few yards from your right elbow. If the murderer shot from there, and then turned the gun across his body and opened it, the ejector might flip the spent case to about there.'

'Not so fast,' Keith said. He handed his gun over to the sergeant, climbed the fence and turned back to whistle Brutus away from the pheasant chicks. He produced the empty cartridge, and the two men studied it together. 'You can often see the imprint of the ejector where the brass base was forced against it at the moment of firing. This one's going rusty, but I'd expect to see it.'

'Depends on the quality of the gun,' the sergeant said. 'In a best gun, the ejectors fit so neatly that there's nothing to make a mark. So we may be looking for somebody with the money to buy a best English game gun.'

'Bad guess,' Keith said. He turned the cartridge and showed two scratches on the brass-coated base. 'Extractor-hooks. This has been fired out of an automatic shotgun, a repeater.'

'It's been fired more than once,' the sergeant pointed out. 'Must've been, if it's been reloaded and fired again. Well, it's a job for the lab and a microscope.' He slipped the cartridge into an old envelope and stowed it in an inner pocket. 'They should be able to match it to a particular gun. If we ever find a particular gun. And if this is the right cartridge. A repeater,' he added thoughtfully, 'ejects the cartridges high, to the right and slightly behind you.'

'Forget it for the moment,' Keith said. 'We don't know

exactly where the cartridge was anyway. We can start thinking again when we've got a gun to think about.'

'I suppose.' The sergeant stared gloomily down the banking. The two hen pheasants were herding their chicks back into cover. 'There'll have to be an inch-by-inch search,' he said. 'Pity Glynder's boys didn't do a thorough job at the time.'

Bearing in mind the seasons of the year, Keith had to agree.

'Onward,' said the sergeant.

Seen close to, Joe Merson's cottage was as well kept as any other building on Mr Grass's property, but paint and cement could not hide the fact that it had been carelessly tenanted. The garden, which had never been cultivated with any enthusiasm, was now a jungle of weeds. Keith thought that it was just the sort of tangle that would attract a pair of partridges, and sure enough his practised eye picked out the hen, sitting tight beneath a canopy of nettles. Keith called Brutus firmly to heel.

Sergeant Yarrow tried the door. 'Unlocked,' he said.

'People don't lock doors much in the country.'

'They do if they're going away for a few months. I'm going to take a look inside.'

Keith circled the outside of the cottage. Brutus followed reluctantly, uneasy. There was an outbuilding at the back which might once have housed a pony. Inside, on a rough but solid bench, were a large paraffin blowlamp, a perforated box of heavy metal, a large and rusty toffee-tin, a plastic carton almost filled with shot, several jamjars of powders and sundry other items of equipment which Keith could identify as being associated with shot-pouring. Beneath the bench was a small stock of scrap lead.

He shouted to the sergeant and received an answer. While

he waited he looked around, deeper into the shadows.

When the sergeant arrived, his face was puckered with distaste. He pounced on some metal bars among the scrap lead. 'Printer's metal? More work for the lab,' he said. 'You wouldn't believe the state of that cottage. Squalid old pig!'

'You'd better come and see this,' Keith said.

A hutch in the corner of the shed held some remains.

'What are . . . were they?'

'Ferrets,' Keith said. 'There were three or four. They were left without food. There was some cannibalism and the last one starved to death.'

'Let's get out of here and find a breath of fresh air.'

Even in the sunshine outside, Keith was still oppressed by the scarecrow atmosphere of the place. The sergeant seemed to feel the same. By tacit agreement they walked back round the cottage and away. They were in an ancient farm-track, overgrown by blackthorn and rowans. When they came out again into the sun it was at the conjunction of four fields. For no better reason than that two of the fields were in crop and the third held bullocks which showed a dangerous interest in Brutus, and, because its gate was the easiest to open, they choose the fourth field, a vacant pasture, and walked aimlessly downhill towards the glint of water half a mile away.

'He wouldn't have left them like that, surely?' the sergeant said.

'Not on purpose. They're attractive little beggars and people get very fond of them – especially antisocial old poachers who live alone. And a man in the village told me that Merson usually left them with him before a trip.'

'He could have asked somebody who let him down.'

'Or was dead. Or thought he was dead. Or he could have got jugged under another name, except that he'd have got a message through somehow, and he doesn't seem to have been the sort of man to bother about covering up his identity. No,' Keith said, 'let's stop kidding ourselves. And let's stay out in the open where we can't be overheard. I'm beginning to get the willies. Let's keep moving.'

They trudged the length of the field in silence and passed through an open gate. 'Subject to the lab confirming the guesses we've been making,' the sergeant said, 'I'm prepared to accept that Mr Grass was shot by somebody else. Accidentally or deliberately, I don't know.'

'Within a few days after that,' Keith said, 'the local poacher disappeared. He left his ferrets to starve. It'll be easy to find out whether this was as uncharacteristic as I think it was.'

They covered a few more yards in silence before the sergeant said, 'Coincidences do happen. Things are happening all the time. It would be extraordinary if none of them ever coincided.'

'It may turn out that way. But, just for the moment, assume that there's a connection. Your local Bobby saw Merson a few days after Mr Grass died. After that, nothing. Do you mind if I theorise?'

'How could I stop you?'

'With difficulty,' Keith said. The two men had dropped into a state of easy friendship which admitted jokey, verbal shorthand. It helped to relieve the disgust that lingered from Merson's cottage and the dead ferrets. 'First, it's possible that Merson shot Mr Grass and then decided to do a bunk. Was there a gun in the cottage?'

'Not that I saw. You didn't give me long for a search. But, if that's how it was, why wait a few days before doing a bunk?'

'It's possible that he thought he was going to be suspected, but, in that case, why has he stayed away? As far as he knows, the whole case is closed.

'Next,' Keith went on, 'it's possible that Merson killed

Grass, and then somebody else killed Merson, possibly out of revenge. I don't like it much, but let's keep it in mind.'

'Let's do that,' the sergeant agreed.

'Then again, there was a rumour, not a very serious one, that the body was Merson's. The evidence as to the identity of the body seems to have been shaky, because of the damage to the face and hands. Would it have been accepted if, say, it had been brought out that another man of roughly the same build and colouring had gone missing?'

'I don't know. I wasn't in the sheriff court when that part of the evidence was given. Probably it wouldn't.'

'There are all kinds of possibilities around that one,' Keith said, 'and I don't like any of them much. The rumours all seemed to be based on the fact that Grass was a bit of a trickster. But his tricks were funny, sometimes malicious, but never serious.' To the sergeant's great amusement, Keith recounted the story of General Winter and the little coloured bubbles. 'Then again,' he went on, 'I helped to sort out some of Grass's personal effects, and I found a box of brand-new lingerie. Not Marks and Sparks but the kind of thing a stripper or a tart wears. The butler was shocked out of his wits when I asked whether Mr Grass went in for that sort of thing. He explained, as if it was the most reasonable thing in the world, that Grass had kept a stock of such trifles for hanging out on the washing-lines of any of the local ladies who happened to have annoyed him, especially if they were away from home for a few days at the time. I gathered that Merson usually did that little job for him. And *that* was the level of Grass's pranks, not swapping blood-stained clothes on corpses.'

'Very speculative,' the sergeant said thoughtfully. 'And inconclusive.'

'Of course it is. I'm not presenting a case to a court, I'm

170

thinking aloud, just hanging a few ideas on you to see if they look good, and at the moment they don't. Somewhere out of the lot, you may get some sort of framework for all the routine investigation that I'll thankfully leave to you.'

'Thanks very much. So your idea of an investigation is to offer me a bunch of wild theories and then leave me to persuade my seniors, who only want me to confirm that it was an accident, that they've got to devote a whole lot of manpower, which is in short supply just now, to doing all the house-to-house enquiries and ground-searches?'

'Now you're getting the idea,' Keith said. 'Except that you – and your bosses – may like the next one a bit better. Let's try introducing a third party from the beginning. Some-body . . . What shall we call him?'

'Jimmy,' said the sergeant.

Keith nodded. There was a trace of Glasgow inflection in the sergeant's voice. In Glasgow, every man is Jimmy until proved otherwise. 'Jimmy is misbehaving himself, round about dusk. Maybe lying in wait for Mr Grass. Maybe poaching – I found evidence of an old poacher's trick not far from where Buggins picked up the cartridge-case. And maybe something quite different.

'Raymond Grass, taking his evening stroll to visit a lady friend, but carrying a gun because it's what men do around here on the off-chance of a crow or a rabbit, arrives at the top of the bank. He may have hung his gun on the fence by the trigger-guard, which is what I often do if I've a fence to climb. That would explain why his hands were empty. He looks down, and there's Jimmy. "What the hell are you doing there, James?" he asks, or words to that effect. Either with what you'd probably call malice aforethought, or else on the spur of the moment, Jimmy brings up his gun. Grass puts his hands over his face. Jimmy lets one off and Grass drops dead. Jimmy doesn't panic. He keeps his head – that's not the happiest expression, but you know what I mean. He arranges things as an accident. If Mr Grass hasn't fired a shot, he'd have to take a chance and let one off from Grass's gun, and risk somebody hearing two shots; but he didn't think to pop one of his own reload's into Grass's gun. Am I boring you?'

'Not a lot,' the sergeant said.

'Good. Now we come to Joe Merson. He was a poacher, and dusk can be a good time for a poacher to be out and about. He could have seen it happen. Or he could have found out some other way. He thinks about it. He's not pleased. He's lost a patron, and no new landlord's likely to thole him and his nasty ways. But he may still be able to profit from it. He thinks it over for a day or two, and then phones Jimmy from the box outside the post office which is where your local cop saw him. He tells Jimmy that he wants umpty pounds, or some other consideration, to keep his mouth shut.

' "All right," Jimmy says. "I'll cough up. Meet me under the blasted oak", or wherever. But Merson's put the figure too high, because Jimmy isn't as prosperous as he looks. So Jimmy, having killed once, decides to do it again, and the shots that Winter says he heard from down this way were Joe Merson to join his crony. How does that grab you?'

'Not exactly by the *habeus corpus*,' the sergeant said. 'It's got more perhapses than a virgin's promise. Who do you have in mind for Jimmy?'

'The general,' Keith said.

Sergeant Yarrow stumbled and recovered himself. 'General *Springburn?* But he's a highly-respected antique!'

'He's also remarkably fit.' Keith thought about the general. 'He could probably walk you or me off our feet. He loads his own cartridges. He's the only person who ever suggested that Grass wasn't always careful with a gun. He's a confirmed poacher –'

'The general? But he was a pal of old Grass. I've seen them around together a hundred times, at functions and things. He must have had permission to shoot here.'

'Only pests,' Keith explained patiently. 'The species that man makes war on, because they multiply successfully in the wild and help themselves to crops. That kind of permission gets given away with a pound of tea provided that the person can be trusted not to take game, which are harvestable species, most of which have to be reared or conserved, and which are an expensive asset and get shot by special invitation only.'

'Perhaps I ought to have known that,' the sergeant admitted, 'but I didn't. I've never been involved in a poaching case.'

'Well, you may have one now. In fact, the more I think about it the more it fits together. The general was certainly helping himself to Mr Grass's pheasants. I think he still is.

'And there's another point. Most of the lessees who're allowed by the will to renew at bargain prices have been nagging Enterkin to get new leases signed as soon as possible. The possibility, rumoured, that Mr Grass might suddenly pop up again may have had something to do with it. Only your own police authorities and the general have been waiting patiently. Wouldn't that suggest that they're the only ones who are quite certain that he's really, truly and finally dead?'

'Circumstantial,' the sergeant said. 'If you offered that as evidence you'd be laughed out of court.'

'Most murder cases are built on circumstantial evidence. I'm only trying to point out where you might be looking for more. It's bloody ironic really. The old soldier, bored by retirement, not exactly well-off on his pension. He gets his kicks and a lot of extra pocket-money by poaching. Like the men in *John Macnab* – have you read it? – he thinks he's risking everything. But, according to Winter, Mr Grass knew all about it. He liked the general so he tolerated it. Grass had made up his mind to have it out with the general. But the general didn't know that his secret was public knowledge. So when Mr Grass's voice suddenly challenges him from the top of the bank his years as a soldier take over. They taught him that life is cheap, firearms are for using and decisions are for making quickly. So he shoots. That's my best theory so far, and if you want to make it less circumstantial you can get your lab comparing firing-pins with that cartridge.'

'Against the general's guns? But we don't even know that it's the right cartridge.'

'I think it's an odds-on shot. But not against the general's guns. Get your hands on the repeater that Winter says the general was trying-out about that time.'

'Got you.' The sergeant slowed to a halt and looked around. 'Since you're doing all the fantasising, try yourself out on this. If you're right, if Jimmy went on to shoot the old poacher, where's the second body?'

'Good God, how should I know?' Keith said. He waved a hand vaguely around at the fields, the woods and the lake. 'I've done the difficult bit. All you've got to do is dig up a few square mile of farmland.'

'Dig up . . .' Sergeant Yarrow roused himself and walked on to the next gate. Keith joined him. The sergeant seemed to have dozed off, his elbows on the top bar of the gate and his chin in his hands. 'No point digging,' he said. 'I was up there,' he nodded across the lake, 'when word came about Mr Grass's death. My God, but it was cold, standing round arguing over some missing sheep when the ground was too

174

hard to have taken any traces at all. And the same was true where Mr Grass died. The ground was too hard to take a mark. We'd had our worst frost of the winter, and it had lasted a fortnight. The ground was frozen to about two feet deep. You couldn't have put a spade in it to bury a body.'

'You could have put him back in his shed,' Keith suggested. 'He'd have kept all right until the thaw came, and then you could bury him in his own garden and wait for the weeds to cover him over.'

'Somebody could come looking for him and find the body. And if you hid him in the undergrowth –'

'The predators would have been starving. The first fox to come by would have found him. And then the carrion crows would have drawn Winter's attention.'

'That's right. If I'd had a body to get rid of,' the sergeant said, 'I'd have put it in the loch.'

'Carry it all that way?'

'All what way? I'd have told old Merson, "Meet me down by the water and I'll give you the money".'

'But the loch would have been frozen over too.'

'Probably. But running water doesn't freeze over so easily. The places where the burns run in and out were probably open. Well, it'd be no use dropping him in at the outflow. But where it runs in, you could push a weighted body under the ice and let the current take it away.'

Keith thought about it. The more he thought, the more reasonable it seemed. 'All right,' he said. 'Let's go and look.'

The sergeant seemed to have taken root. 'I think I've walked far enough for one day,' he said.

Keith had walked further. He remembered his debilitated state. 'So've I,' he said. 'Let's go back to the inn, have a pint and you can phone for frogmen.'

After a few seconds spent wrestling with temptation, the

sergeant shook his head. 'If I call out the frogmen and there's nothing there, I'll be back in uniform and lecturing the schools on road safety. I'd better take a look. If nothing else, I can get the scene clear in my mind.'

Keith sighed. 'Let's get it over,' he said. 'This way.'

Although they were walking round the lake they could hardly see the water for the trees and undergrowth, except at the small creek where the boathouse stood, until they came to a half-acre of open grass at the mouth of the feeder stream. As they approached the stream, Brutus sensed the interest which they were taking in the ground and intensified his own hunting, to and fro, until he pounced on a small object in the grass.

'Here you are,' Keith said. 'Another cartridge.'

'There must be thousands lying around.'

'Well, I don't see any. I've never seen but the two.'

'That's because you've stopped noticing them except when they've got a special meaning for you.'

'No,' Keith said, 'it's because Winter's such a bloody tyrant about always taking your cartridges home with you that I think even the two poachers would rather have been caught poaching than dropping a cartridge.'

Brutus was nudging Keith's leg. He stooped, and the dog delivered another object into his hand. It was a lower dental plate.

'Please,' the sergeant said, 'don't ask me if I think there are thousands of these lying around. I couldn't stand sarcasm just now. Let's look around.'

They searched around the mouth of the stream, casting both ways along the banks, but even with Brutus' help they found nothing more of interest.

'You wouldn't expect to find many traces,' Keith said. 'Not all these weeks after a crime that was committed in a black frost anyway.'

176

'Probably not. But there'll have to be a search. I'm going to be popular with the rank-and-file. It'll be pouring wet. It always is when that sort of miserable job has to be done.'

'What a terrible shame,' Keith said absently. 'The poor laddies. My heart bleeds. This is just about where I'd drop a body in, if I had one I wanted rid of. You can see how the spate must come down in winter. Where we're standing would be under water, but shallow enough to wade. I'd weight a body with stones, or whatever couldn't be traced to me. The force of the water would take it under the ice and out into deeper water where it'd run slower.' He threw a stick in and watched it float away. 'That's about the line it would follow, and if it didn't get snagged up I'd expect it to settle down between twenty and fifty yards out, depending on the current and how heavily the body was weighted. Right. That's solved your problem for you. Now can we go and get some lunch?'

'You're joking,' said the sergeant.

'No I'm not. Come back with a frogman or two, and I believe you've got a sixty-forty chance of finding a corpse where I said. And I'll tell you something else. It won't be Mr Grass, because his teeth were all his own.'

'As a jumper to conclusions, you're Grand National material. Anybody could have fumbled and dropped his lower choppers, or sneezed them out. And if the ground was flooded at the time he wouldn't have a hope of finding them again. Especially if he didn't have your highly trained denture-hound with him at the time,' the sergeant said. 'And I meant you were joking about giving up now. You can't just stand there theorising about real people and real bodies and then walk away. Is there a boat in that boathouse?'

Keith had been carried along by the momentum of his own reasoning and by the various discoveries which could be considered to support it. The sudden intrusion of reality chilled him. 'Haven't we gone far enough already?' he suggested. 'We seem to be tramping about all over any evidence there may be. Should you go dragging lakes on your own authority?'

'I don't see why not. There won't be any footprints on the loch. I'm getting hungry myself, but I can't row a boat and drag the bottom as well, so I'll be obliged for your help.'

'All right,' Keith said against his better judgement.

EIGHTEEN

The boathouse was locked, but they found the key under a slate beside the door and entered the tar-smelling gloom. The larger boat was out of the water but a robust plywood dinghy was afloat, complete with oars. Keith hid his gun under a thwart of the other boat rather than risk it on the water, and they were ready.

The sergeant took the oars, with Keith in the stern nursing a grapnel which they had found hanging inside the boat-house door. Brutus ran to and fro on the bank and then settled down, whining but yet relieved at being excused from an outing which he regarded as alien and therefore probably doomed.

Sergeant Yarrow soon mastered the knack of the oars, and a few minutes took them back to the head of the loch. The sergeant dipped his oars so that the boat would follow the deeper current, and Keith lowered the grapnel until he could feel its hooks brushing the muddy bottom.

Families of mallard, which had scattered when they came out, became used to their intrusion and paddled almost under the oars.

They had time to look around. From this low level, the panorama was of woods and hedges with hardly a field visible until the ground rose in the middle distance, but somewhere there was the sound of a tractor. Keith could see the upper half of Whinkirk House and the roofs of some of the houses beyond, and most of Wellhead Farm on its hill.

From time to time the grapnel brought up debris from the

bottom or clumps of a weed that Keith thought was stone-wort, and once, on their third drift down, it snagged on something immoveable and it took ten minutes of prodding with an oar to free it. On their fifth drift, it caught in something that moved sluggishly.

'Hold your horses,' Keith said. 'I'm into something.'

The sergeant backed water gently, to hold the boat steady.

Keith pulled in the line until the grapnel was only a few inches below the surface. It was caught in a grey nylon anorak of popular style, the pockets of which were dragged down by something loose and heavy. The remains of a face stared sightlessly through the water and over his shoulder.

'Oh my God!' he said. 'I never really believed it.'

'Can you hold on to it while I pull for the shore?' Sergeant Yarrow asked.

'Hang on a moment,' Keith said shakily. 'This needs a bit of thinking over.' He made sure that the grapnel had a good hold on the corpse's clothing and then let the line out gently until the bottom was reached again. The boat revolved slowly until it lay to the body as if to an anchor.

'What's the hangup now? I want to report this. And you were starving to death a few minutes ago.'

Keith dipped his hands into the cold water and then put them to his face. 'Can't you wait to get back and tell your boss what a pig's breakfast Glynder made of the first investigation?'

The sergeant thought over the question. 'No,' he said.

'If you want to be sure of getting that pleasure, you'd better think about this. We've been a wee bit rash, but let's not make it worse. Consider this. What I just brought up wasn't Mr Grass. It had no teeth in the bottom jaw, and he had all his own. We now seem to have two murders, with strong local connections. Right?'

The sergeant nodded.

'This is a place where gossip travels faster than the jungle drums. I've been asking pointed questions. The murderer must know that. Do you not think Jimmy would keep an eye and an ear open, to know what I'm up to?'

The sergeant nodded again.

'So what does he see? He sees me pay a visit to the police. A few days later, a C.I.D. sergeant meets me at the inn. We walk to the place of the first murder. Then we go to the second victim's house and probably behave like a couple of the stars of the silent screen who've been told to register excitement and horror. Well, if our Jimmy saw or heard of only a part of all this, by now he's either watching us through binoculars or stalking us through the woods. And what do we do? Talking all the way, we walk in the direction of the second victim's body. We examine the place where the body was dumped and pocket another two clues. Then we get in a boat, row out into the lake and can be presumed to find the second body.

'Now, let's go on looking at it from Jimmy's viewpoint. If there's nothing to connect him with Mr Grass's murder, then none of us has anything to worry about. But if there's any connection, so that the finding of the second body, with the very strong inference that Grass died by murder, is dangerous to Jimmy, then the non-discovery of the second body may be very important to him.'

'I don't think I like your reasoning as much as I did,' the sergeant said.

'Keep your voice down. You know how sound travels over water. In Jimmy's shoes, I might decide that two more mysterious disappearances or accidents, or one of each, would be better than having Joe Merson found. The weather's much more suitable for a little grave-digging than it was in February, and the evidence would soon be grown over. I'd think that I had nothing to lose and might have everything to gain.'

Sergeant Yarrow bit his lower lip. 'It's all ifs and ands and buts again,' he said.

'True. But that's what you said last time.'

'And I don't go for this domino effect in murders. Some faceless Jimmy wandering around knocking off half the countryside. The idea's like something out of bad television.'

Before staking his life, Keith preferred to calculate the odds. 'Would you say that nobody ever killed again to cover up a first crime?' he asked.

'You know it happens,' the sergeant said irritably. 'Not often, but sometimes.'

'Now put yourself in a murderer's place. Be Jimmy for a moment. If you had killed once and then killed again to cover up the first killing, and then found that your secret was again in danger, would you find it more difficult to kill yet again? Or would it get a wee bit easier every time?'

The sergeant's only answer was a visible shiver.

They looked around. The near countryside presented an uncaring, leafy face. The few visible fields were empty and even the tractor's engine had stopped or died away. 'A few years ago,' Keith said, 'these fields would've been fairly teeming with men. The face of farming's changed, and not for the better.'

'Never mind griping, go on being the murderer. I don't like it, I don't necessarily believe it, but you seem to have the knack.'

'Do you ever get the feeling that you're being watched?' Keith asked.

'No, never.'

'Nor do I. That's what worries me. A man, or a dozen men,

could be watching me through telescopic sights, and I wouldn't know. If I was Jimmy, I'd be lurking somewhere in all that undergrowth. I might wait near the boathouse, to catch us on our way back. But watching us sitting here and arguing, I could make a damn good guess at what we're saying. And I'd have to try and guess which side we'd come ashore, because, the loch being longer than it's wide and with the banks overgrown beside, it'd be quicker to row across than to run round.'

'And anything we think, he can think too and try to go one better,' the sergeant said unhappily. 'So it's just a toss of the coin and a brief prayer that there's only one of him. I wish we'd never had this conversation at all.'

'Between you and me, my prayer is that there aren't any of him just here and now.'

'I'll second that. Now, be the murderer again. What would you think if you saw the boat being rowed very slowly towards one bank?'

'I would guess,' Keith said slowly, 'that it was a bluff and that we were going to row back very quickly towards the opposite bank.'

'Right. You can switch off now, I've made up my mind. I'm going to row very slowly towards the boat house, and hope that he'll start for the other side. Then, when we get within fifty yards or so, I'm going to pull like hell and we'll go straight inside and grab your gun.' The sergeant bent to his oars and pulled slowly for the boat-house.

'About that prayer of yours,' Keith said. 'Would you care to add a brief request that he doesn't have a rifle and that my gun's still there?'

'No point repeating myself,' the sergeant said, 'I just *did* that one. Now I'm praying that I'm as good a guesser as you are, and better than he is.'

'Amen.'

183

Leaving the sunken body behind, they moved slowly towards the boat-house. Keith scanned the banks. There was no sign of movement in either direction, but an army could have moved unseen behind that cover. Keith thought that there probably wasn't anybody there anyway. He thought that if some innocent bird-watcher appeared suddenly on the bank, somebody was going to need a clean pair of underpants.

Fifty yards from the bank, the sergeant rested on his oars. 'Any sign?'

Keith tried to look into the silent foliage. 'Nothing.'

'Here we go, then.'

The sergeant pulled like an Olympic oarsman. The light dinghy rose in the water. It went faster than Keith could have believed. They were even overtaking a fleeing moorhen. Yet the boat-house seemed to be coming no nearer. Keith made up his mind that, at the first sign of danger, he was going to get underwater in one jump.

At the very mouth of the creek, a short stone's-throw from the boat-house, there wept a great willow-tree. It stood slightly back from the bank so that the circle of dangling fronds barely reached the water. The boat was entering the creek, almost abreast of the willow, when Keith's eye was drawn to Brutus. He was sitting by the tree, patiently waiting, staring into its dark interior.

Keith wondered whether some animal, perhaps a feral mink, was in there. But Brutus' tail was sweeping the grass.

And Keith remembered: Brutus would follow the man with the gun. 'There's someone inside the willow,' he hissed.

It was too late to retreat. While Keith was still wondering what the hell to do, the sergeant pulled hard on one oar, swinging the dinghy straight for the tree.

Everything seemed to happen in the flick of an eye.

The sergeant gave one more mighty pull on the oars.

Keith let himself fall backwards into the bottom of the boat.

The sergeant turned and sprang in one movement, launching himself in what should have been a flying tackle through the branches. It was a brave act and might have been suicidal. But the thrust of his leap shot the dinghy backwards from under him.

The shot came, with the ringing blast that can only be heard in front of the muzzles.

The sergeant landed in three feet of water and two of mud.

Keith was looking past his own feet into a hole that had been blown in the foliage. He could see the muzzles of a shotgun and a pale blur behind that might have been a face and a pair of hands. He seemed to be looking right down the barrels and counting the pellets. The echoes of the first shot were not dead, and he could hear duck taking off, disturbed by the unseasonable sound.

Fascinated, he watched the twin muzzles that looked so like the eye-sockets of a skull, and waited for them to sound his knell.

There was a loud pop, and suddenly the air was filled with little coloured bubbles. And then he bumped the bank on the other side of the creek. He could hear the sound of someone crashing away through the bracken and brambles.

'Of course it was the bloody general,' Keith said. He peered out of the boat-house door, gun in hand, like some settler waiting for the Indians. 'Old Grass mixed some trick cartridges with his. I told you. They just went pop and blew out a lot of coloured bubbles.'

'Is that what happened? I was underwater at the time. When I came up, I wondered why you were still alive.'

'That's exactly what happened. I was looking right down his barrels – it was a side-by-side – and suddenly we had bath-night in Technicolor. And as for you,' Keith stirred the soaking wet Brutus with his foot, 'I'm trying to believe you took to the water to help me. But in my heart I know that what you were after was to retrieve me. You don't give a damn, do you?'

'It needn't have been the general. You said people swap cartridges, as if I didn't know it. But you heard whoever-it-was run off?' the sergeant asked anxiously.

'Yes. That's not to say that he isn't going to wait for us somewhere else. We'd better stay as much in the open as we can. You coming?'

'You think I'm staying here while you take the gun away? Of course I'm coming.'

Outside the boathouse, the world looked abnormally normal. It was only when they stepped outside that Keith saw the blood on the other's hand. 'He hit you?'

Sergeant Yarrow nodded. 'He got my shoulder. At that ramge, I don't know how he didn't blow my arm off.'

'Come on.'

As soon as they were back in the fields and safe from immediate ambush Keith stopped and made the sergeant take his soaking jacket off. 'About twenty pellets,' he said, 'not too deep. Shooting through leaves and twigs must have scattered his pattern and you just caught the fringe. You were bloody lucky.'

'We both were,' Yarrow said. 'Where are we heading?'

'The village.'

They set off again, avoiding thick cover and ignoring crops and cattle. Keith thought of things that he would do to the general. He wondered whether shooting people while not wearing a white coat would contravene the terms of the will.

'How're the wounds holding up?' he asked.

'Not bad. It's my feet that're bothering me.'

'He shot you in them?'

'You've walked me off them.'

Where their path plunged into the woods that backed the village, they paused. 'Good place for an ambush,' said the sergeant.

Keith had opened his mouth to reply when a shot sounded, loud and near. He bit his tongue. The sergeant jumped several inches and uttered a word of startling vulgarity. Each looked at the other and was surprised to find him alive.

Brutus' reaction was quite different. He darted forward and pinned a still kicking rabbit.

Miss Wyper stepped out of the trees, shotgun hanging negligently over her arm. 'Sorry if I startled you. I didn't see you coming.' She took the rabbit from Brutus and dispatched it with a flick of her wrist. 'That's clobbered the bastard,' she said cheerfully. 'Three more for a hat and I'm ready.'

Keith held his own gun two-handed. It was against his instincts to point it at a lady, but he kept it where he could bring it to bear instantly. 'Has the general passed this way?' he asked.

'I haven't seen a soul,' she said. She looked at them curiously. The sergeant had taken up position behind Keith, who was backing slowly away from her.

'My − er − friend fell in the loch and hurt himself,' Keith said. 'Got to get on. Need doctor. Good hunting!'

'Just a minute,' the sergeant said. 'Have you been down by the loch?'

She shook her head. 'I've been in the village, posting

yesterday's letters. Cheerio!' She strode off in the direction of Whinkirk House.

The two men stood taking deep breaths. 'I didn't really suspect her anyway,' Keith said shakily.

'Nor did I,' said the sergeant. He came out from behind Keith.

Their way brought them into the village by a path that led between the gardens of a row of cottages. A plump figure was pulling vegetables in one of the gardens and Keith recognised the comely barmaid from the inn. She looked up, recognised him, started to smile and then saw the colour of the sergeant's face and the blood on his hand.

'Whatever's happened?' she asked, and, without waiting for an answer, 'you'd better come inside quick.'

'Do you have a phone?'

'No. But the doctor's visiting two doors away. I can fetch him.'

'Fine,' Keith said. 'And I'll go and borrow him some dry clothes.'

Inside the cottage, a stout figure had been sleeping off a heavy lunch on Penny's sofa. Mr Enterkin sat up, blinking.

'So this is where you've been skiving off to,' Keith said.

'No it is not,' Mr Enterkin said truculently. He rubbed the sleep out of his face. 'And I haven't been skiving off. And . . . and what the hell's going on? Did you shoot this man?'

'No I did not. The blasted general did it.'

'That he didn't,' said Penny Laing. 'The general was taken off to hospital this morning. Took ill in the night, poor soul.'

NINETEEN

Keith walked to the inn. Quite illegally, he carried his loaded gun at the ready. Nobody seemed to notice. It was most of an hour before he returned. The largest part of that time was spent on the phone to the police, relaying a series of messages from Sergeant Yarrow to several of his superiors, answering questions and receiving messages in return. A few minutes were enough for borrowing a change of clothing from Harvey Brown. The rest of the time was spent in trying to find reverse on the sergeant's car, which was a model strange to him. He found it after much trial and many errors, and drove back to Penny's cottage.

He found the sergeant stripped to the waist in front of a comforting fire, heavily bandaged around the left shoulder and admiring a wine-glass which contained a number of shotgun pellets. 'Home-poured,' he said. 'They look as if they may have come from Joe Merson.'

There was a mixed grill waiting on the table for Keith, with a can of beer. 'Sergeant Jim said you hadn't had anything to eat since breakfast,' Penny told him. 'He's already had his.'

'That's no way to refer to an officer,' Enterkin said from the couch. He had resumed his prone position. 'If you must fraternise with the rival branch of the law, show a proper respect.'

'He asked me to call him Jim,' Penny explained.

Keith found that he was hungrier than he could remember ever being. As he ate, he could hear the sergeant

189

protesting his outraged modesty in the room next door as Penny helped him to change into Harvey Brown's dry clothes. She came back and snatched Keith's plate away as soon as it was empty. 'That silly boy,' she said. 'He can't move his arm, but he won't be helped. Take a scone.'

'You'll make me fat,' Keith said, helping himself.

She considered him, her head on one side. 'A little more weight would suit you,' she said. 'Your wife doesn't feed you enough. I'm the one that needs to get some weight off.'

'Nonsense.'

'Just pleasantly plump,' Enterkin said sleepily.

The sergeant rejoined them, dry-clad but ill-fitted. 'We can talk in front of Mrs Laing,' he said. 'She wheedled the story out of me anyway. What did my chiefs have to say?'

Keith thought back. 'If you need to go to hospital —'

'I don't.'

'— I'm to take you there. But if you've had adequate medical attention for the moment, you're to wait at the inn while the body's secured or a guard put on the loch. When that's all in hand, somebody'll come and drive you home. But would you radio in, if you have one with you, or phone if you don't and confirm what I said to them just in case I'm a hoaxer.'

'If I'd had a radio on me I'd still be out in the middle of the loch screaming for help. Did I seem to be unpopular?'

'Glynder wasn't too pleased,' Keith said. 'But your own chief seemed to be delighted. There doesn't seem to be much love lost between him and Glynder.'

'Not a lot.'

'We'd better be getting round to the inn,' Penny broke in. 'You can talk there. Mrs Brown's away, and if the bars open late there'll be thirsty men battering on the doors.'

'I'll be one of them,' said Sergeant Jim. 'I've suddenly developed the most colossal thirst, and I can hardly be on

190

duty and I can't drive. The inn's a good place to wait. And I seem to remember that they have a very pretty barmaid there with a lovely bosom.'

Keith and Penny exchanged a wink. 'Shame on you,' Mr Enterkin said. 'She's old enough to be your mother.'

'I am not,' Penny said.

The sergeant began to blush furiously.

Like most men, the sergeant was a bad passenger in his own car. They were all glad when the inn was reached. In the cool of the empty private bar the three men took stools while Penny Laing busied herself with the routine of opening up. Brutus, still damp, flopped by the dead fireplace.

'I could have sworn that it was the general,' Keith said glumly.

'Well, it wasn't,' Penny said.

'Everything pointed to him. How old's your Glen Grant?' Keith asked. On being satisfied that the malt whisky was of a respectable age he decided to accept a dram. 'Those cartridges alone . . .'

'Export,' said Sergeant Jim.

'Pint?'

'If you've nothing larger. You don't know that those are the important cartridges.'

'Colin Winter's as fussy as an old wife about cartridges lying around, and those are the only two I've ever seen, and they were both fired from a repeater.'

'I seem doomed,' Mr Enterkin began, 'to spend my evening listening to, and possibly participating in, forlorn speculation on a subject which holds for me no profit and therefore very little interest. I see no reason to remain more clear-headed than my company. I shall have a large brandy. With soda.' He produced a five-pound note. 'And you'll oblige me by taking the round out of this.'

Penny put a jug of water beside Keith's whisky. 'You didn't say anything about a repeating shotgun,' she said accusingly to the sergeant. 'And the general doesn't have one of those.'

'How would you know that?' the sergeant asked.

'She knows everything,' said Enterkin proudly.

'He was trying one out back in February,' Keith said. 'Colin Winter told me.'

'Colin's wrong, then.' Penny said, topping up the pint glass. 'The general was trying it out early in January, because I remember him saying that he was thinking of giving himself a late Christmas present. But he never bought it. You see, the inn's a sort of market-place. Most private deals get settled in here. Colin bought the gun himself, later.'

'That's funny,' Keith said. 'I wonder why he didn't tell me that it was the same gun.'

'Was there any reason that he should?'

'I suppose not.'

'I'd better phone in,' said Sergeant Jim. 'Can I have some change?'

'Don't bother with the phone-box,' Penny said. She lifted a telephone from under the bar and put it on the counter.

'Bless you! I don't know that I'll ever recover enough strength to get off this stool.' The sergeant dialled his number.

'All this walking's very debilitating,' Enterkin said sympathetically.

Keith was determined to stick to one subject. 'Unless there's something we don't know about,' he said, 'I can't see any motive for Colin Winter to do such a thing.'

'What thing?' asked Penny.

'Kill Mr Grass. He was the other person who was likely to see us hiking around the place and skilled enough to follow us without being spotted. And he had the repeater.'

'Not when Mr Grass died, he didn't. He only bought it about a month ago.'

Keith was silenced. Vaguely aware of Sergeant Jim's voice on the telephone, he was reviewing people and guns. If he were wrong in his interpretation of the faint marks on the cartridges . . .

'I'll hang on,' the sergeant was saying. He covered the mouthpiece. 'There's another panic on,' he told them. 'A hit-and-run driver. It seems to have been deliberate, she was run over more than once by something fairly heavy. That's all they can say, so far.'

'Who?' they asked in unison.

'A Mrs Ambrose. Almost outside her own house. Quite dead.'

Keith's first reaction was regret, that an attractive, sensual woman had departed the world unenjoyed by himself. Then pity for the crippled husband whose wife, however faithless, had at least stayed by him. And then irritation. Mrs Ambrose had been his next choice – the woman of a certain age, saddled with an impotent husband, ridding herself of the old lover to spend his money on the new. He had wondered whether the Ambroses had been considering a repeater for their son. But if this last death were connected with the others . . .

Penny had been staring into a glass that she was polishing, as if it had been a crystal ball. 'But that's awful,' she said suddenly. She had turned very pale. 'Wicked! She really is old enough to be his mother. Well, nearly.' The three men gaped at her. 'Don't look at me like that. Get onto them quickly. Tell them to go to Wellhead Farm, real quick, and to watch the car-washes and places like that. Tell them they must look at Mrs Benton's Land Rover before she has time to wash it off.'

193

'Wash what off?'

'I don't know. Blood. Hair. Skin. Bits of clothes. Whatever it is that you find on a car that's knocked somebody down.'

The sergeant had caught up with her. 'I have a tip from an informant,' he said. Briskly, without a wasted word, he began to relay Penny's advice.

The influx was arriving in the public bar and Penny went through to serve. The sergeant, still speaking on the phone, was making signals to Keith who, hoping that he was interpreting them correctly, got up and put a chair under the handle of each door. The private bar was going to remain especially private that evening.

Penny returned through the back-bar door just as the sergeant hung up the phone. 'There's a car on the way to the farm,' he said. 'I'll get a call as soon as they know anything.'

'And the car-washes?' asked Penny.

'There's only two within miles. They're going to be out of order from now on. But,' Sergeant Jim asked plaintively, 'you mean that Mrs Benton killed Mrs Ambrose? On purpose?'

Penny picked up another glass to polish. 'Of course, my dear.'

'And Mr Grass, and Joe Merson?'

'Yes.'

'Let's have your reasoning.'

The brief flush of confidence had deserted Penny. 'It's not reasoning that I could give you in a logical order. It's just a lot of things,' she said shyly. 'Things. Do you know what I mean? Things that I knew anyway. What you told me this afternoon set me wondering. When you said that about the repeating shotgun, it began to come together. But, before I spoke out, I stopped to wonder who else was in danger if it was Mrs Benton. And I'd just decided that there were two people, and

194

Mrs Ambrose was one of them, when you said she'd been knocked down and killed.'

There was an impatient knocking from the public bar. 'If you think Mr Grass and old Joe were killed with a repeater,' she said quickly, 'I may as well tell you that Mrs Benton used to own the gun that the general tried out in January and Colin bought later. She was sitting where you are, Sergeant Jim, when the deal was done.' She slipped away through the back-bar door.

'Purple scented mouse-crap!' Sergeant Jim exploded. 'She can't just tell us that somebody else's neck's on the chopping-block and then buzz off!'

'She just did,' Keith said.

The sergeant ducked under the flap in the bar counter and went in pursuit. Craning his neck, Keith could see an excited conversation being pursued in whispers. The sergeant returned, ducked back and resumed his stool. 'She says not to worry, there's no danger now. She can't really be that far ahead of us, can she? A woman?' He was engaged to marry a feather-brained filing-clerkess and confidently expected to live happily ever after.

'Her reasoning powers are better than she gives herself credit for,' Enterkin said anxiously. He had never married, but had enjoyed a protracted affair with a lady possessed of acute reasoning powers, and had sometimes had cause to feel that where the female I.Q. was concerned enough was enough. 'She's nobody's fool. And she had a flying start over any of us. Anything of importance that is said or done in this village is said or done in the bar here, or talked over in the bar afterwards.'

The phone rang and the sergeant picked it up and listened. Penny came through the back-bar door and raised her eyebrows. The sergeant ignored her, but on a signal from Keith she refilled the glasses.

Sergeant Jim laid down the phone with a satisfied nod. 'That does it,' he said. 'One of the cars *en route* for the loch was diverted to Wellhead Farm. They found the lady running out her hose. Blood and hair on her Land Rover. She's now said to be helping us with our enquiries, but not, I understand, helping one hell of a lot.'

'She didn't strike me as the helpful type,' Keith said. 'Now, for God's sake, Penny, tell us how you knew. But don't tell us that gossip had her pegged for it all the time.'

'Not exactly.' Penny paused, and a mild frown disturbed her soft brow. 'I think I fancy a brandy and ginger,' she said. She looked at Keith. He pushed another pound note across the bar. She mixed her drink and gave him his change before she went on. 'One thing was this. I wondered who could have noticed the two of you prowling around and finding Joe Merson's remains. I know the lie of the land there. Before he died, my husband used to rent grazing off the Bentons, and from Wellhead Farm you get a view of the loch and all over. And I've seen her with binoculars. Would she know your face, Sergeant Jim?'

'I was interviewing her when the news of Mr Grass's death came in. She'd complained about sheep-stealing. It turned out to be holes in the fence.'

'There you are, then. And I wondered who might have reason to wish Mr Grass away, and I thought of her again. A whole lot of people are better off for being left his money and things, but only one was on the edge of bankruptcy. She has debts the way a hedgehog has fleas..'

'Not easy to lose money at farming these days,' Keith said.

'Well, she and her husband, they had the knack of it. I've heard the seedsmen and suppliers talking, she'd no credit left at all. She married beneath her, of course, and her family gave her the farm to get rid of them both. Only four hundred acres it was then, and they borrowed a whole lot of money to buy the rest when it came on the market. And both of them living it up, hunters and point-to-points and gambling.

'And then her husband died and left her his debts, and of course men aren't so keen to give credit to a woman in farming.

'She couldn't make a go of it on her own. In a farming community, there's always talk about what's the best crops for next year and where the best prices'll be and what the EEC'll do to them next, and somehow between them they usually come to the right decisions. But she and her husband, they'd never mixed with the farming crowd, thought they were one better, so she never got the benefit. Always making wrong guesses, she was, so the farmers were saying in here. And now the land's all let for grazing, and the men were adding it up in the bar and reckoning that she couldn't be taking in more than'd pay the interest on her loans.'

'She could have sold up,' Keith said.

'But she needed something behind her. Since her husband died, she'd been setting her cap at Bert Yates, over at North Farm. Young Mr Yates, I mean.'

'I didn't think you meant the old man,' Keith said. He remembered Mrs Ambrose with Bert Yates. He felt his face glow.

'Stranger things have happened,' Penny said. Absently, she mixed herself another drink and looked around for the money. 'She seems to fancy the farmers,' she said.

'Whereas you go more for solicitors,' said the sergeant, taking out his wallet. 'Set them up again,' he added.

'That's right.' She winked. 'There's a lot of old nonsense talked about farmers. Solicitors have more spunk to them.'

Mr Enterkin felt that if he were not turning pink then he

should be. 'Go on about Mrs Benton,' he said.

'It was to get a place of his own Bert Yates was after,' she said. 'That stuck out a mile. He wanted to get away from that father of his, and who could blame him? But when he realised that she'd got nothing of her own he seemed to decide that he'd be better off staying by his dad and waiting for the old man to pop off, and in the meantime he took up with Mrs Ambrose. And I don't suppose it was money he was after . . .'

'Is that why she was killed?' asked the sergeant. 'Jealousy?'

'That maybe made it easier but it wasn't the whole of it, not by any manner of means. I'll come to that. Let me finish about Mrs Benton first. I heard her speaking to Mr Grass one day about six months ago, sitting in here. She was taking a sherry, same as himself, although she usually preferred gin. Trying to please him, I thought at the time. She didn't let on as she was broke, too proud for that, and I don't suppose he knew it for he was never one to listen to gossip. She tried to lease him her shooting rights or to sell him a bit of land. But he said that he'd got more than enough to be going on with. Then he said that he hoped that her land'd be added to his some day, and I saw her begin to light up, but he went on to say that he'd made provison in his will for her land to be bought in for a good sum of money. "More than it'd fetch on the open market," he says, "but I shan't feel like haggling by then". So she knew she had enough coming to save her bacon when he was gone.

'And while I was remembering about that,' Penny went on, 'I was wondering who could do such a thing. There's a few around here that you'd think were ruthless. Most have a soft streak somewhere. But not her. She's the first to shoot a dog that's worrying sheep, even a pet poodle once that was only wanting to play. And it's more than that sort of thing.

It's the feeling you get when you see and hear somebody. I don't know what it is, but you can tell.

'One more thing. You said about cartridges being passed from hand to hand, and it made me wonder who'd been shooting with the general. And I remembered the general saying that Mrs Benton was a pretty good shot, for a woman.'

Thirsty voices were calling from the other bar and she went through to attend to them.

'It's not who you know, it's what you know,' said the sergeant. 'If we'd had a tenth of her local knowledge between us . . . I think I'll make friends with every barmaid for fifty miles around.'

'Sounds like fun,' Keith said. 'I'll come with you.'

The sergeant was scribbling frantically in a notebook. 'I'd better get all this down,' he said. 'With a little editing, I can make myself out to be the greatest detective of all time.'

'Well, make a note of this,' Keith said. 'It explains the noise of a tractor that I heard while we were down at the loch.'

'I heard it too.'

They sat in silence until Mr Enterkin said, 'I've just realised that we've as much right as anyone else to bang on the bar,' and he rapped with a large ashtray.

Penny came back at last. 'Same again, is it?' she asked.

'That is not why we called you back,' said Mr Enterkin, 'and very well you know it.'

'We can't afford your prices,' said the sergeant.

She smiled softly. 'Have one with me,' she said, and started pouring.

'And now,' said the sergeant, '*dear* Mrs Laing, please tell us why Mrs Ambrose was on the hate-list.'

'All right.' Penny finished serving, and carefully counted money from her purse into the till. 'Mr Brown's in next door now, so we needn't be interrupted again. I'll tell you. It was something that happened in here.'

'It would be,' said the sergeant. 'Go on.'

'It was a Friday. That's the day most of the ladies do their shopping for the weekend, and some of them pop in here for a drink and a chat before lunch. There were three of them in here that day, Mrs Ambrose, Mrs Benton and a Mrs Burns. It was about ten days after Mr Grass died, perhaps a week after Joe Merson went missing, and they'd been talking about whether the one thing had anything to do with the other. Mrs Ambrose said to Mrs Benton, in that snooty voice of hers, "I thought Joe had moved in with you, dear." Mrs Benton turned scarlet and asked her what she meant. Well, I was called through to the other bar and I didn't hear all that Mrs Ambrose said. But I heard a bit of it. Mrs Ambrose said something about a crossed line. Then she said, "I heard you make a date . . ." That was all.'

Sergeant Jim made a silent whistle. 'It was enough,' he said. 'If Mrs Benton knew that Mrs Ambrose had heard her invite Joe Merson to meet her down by the loch, then the moment that his body was found Mrs Ambrose became a ticking bomb. I suppose the other one in danger was this Mrs Burns.'

'No, dear. She was in the little girls' room when that was said. I meant me,' Penny said. 'I heard it too.'

Mr Enterkin dropped his glass. 'Oh my God!' he said, in a squeak that was far from his usual booming voice. 'There was a Land Rover outside your cottage.'

Penny patted his hand. 'I know,' she said gently. 'I saw it as we were getting into Sergeant Jim's car. But don't take on about it.' She leaned across the bar and kissed Mr Enterkin on the chubby cheek. 'It's all over now.'

Silence fell while each of them thought of what might

have been. Somebody rattled the door-knob, gave up and went away.

The sergeant looked up from a fresh page of scribbles. 'One more question,' he said. 'And if any of you can answer it I'll buy the next round, and you can make it Champagne if you like.'

'I don't think I'll serve you three any more,' Penny said. 'I think you've had enough.'

The sergeant ignored her. 'The question's this. We can prove that Mrs Benton's Land Rover killed Mrs Ambrose. We can probably prove that she was driving it at the time. But a good Q.C. might easily get her off lightly, as a hit-and-run driver who'd panicked after the victim carelessly stepped off the kerb under her wheels. We can infer that she killed Mr Grass and Joe Merson, but these are inferences backed up by the most slender of circumstantial evidence. Can anybody provide me with the least bit of hard, physical proof?'

Silence fell again. Mr Enterkin stirred at last. 'I suppose it's my turn to buy the drinks,' he said.

'Just a minute,' Penny said. 'Don't you go giving up so easy.' She planted her elbows on the bar in front of the sergeant. 'If I give you the answer, will you give me a bottle of Champagne, to put by for my next wedding?'

The sergeant dragged his eyes away from her cleavage. 'Gladly. And I'll come and help you drink it.'

'I'll be fair with you,' she said. 'What I'm going to tell you is going to come out anyway, because it's not a thing can be hid.'

The sergeant poised his pencil. 'That doesn't matter to me,' he said. 'I want to be able to take in a case with proof.'

'All right. You know the bits of it between you anyway. It's just that you don't know the same bits. I'll ask you some

201

questions, just as if I was a real lawyer in court.'

'Before you start,' Enterkin said, 'put up another round of drinks, so that we can listen in comfort. I need something, after that shock. You're called to the other bar, in fact.'

'All right.' Penny turned to the bottles but spoke over her shoulder. 'Sergeant Jim, you looked through Joe Merson's cottage?'

'I did.'

'Did you see his gun there? It was an old single-barrel hammer-gun.'

'No, M'Lud, I didn't. It's probably at the bottom of the loch. Maybe parts of it were used to help weight him down.'

'Don't go jumping ahead, now. If you were trying to blackmail somebody, and he or she said to come down to a lonely place at dusk to meet them, and you had a gun, would you take it along with you?'

'I'd be a fool not to,' the sergeant said.

'And if you realised, all of a sudden, that the other person was going to try and kill you?'

'I'd try to get my shot off first.'

'Exactly! Now, Sergeant Jim, tell me this. When you were interviewing her about the missing sheep, did you notice her feet?'

'Her *feet?*'

'Now your getting it, my dear.'

'Don't call him your dear,' Enterkin said. 'You'll spoil the judicial atmosphere. And make me jealous.'

'Your turn in a minute,' Penny said.

'She certainly had feet,' the sergeant said thoughtfully. 'Two of them. Yes, I remember. Quite small, in brogues.'

'She was walking about?'

'Striding around like an Amazon.'

202

'Now, my dear,' Penny said to Enterkin. 'You've been up to see her about the will?'

'What a relief,' Enterkin said, 'to know that you can be wrong. Keith went to see her.'

Penny switched her gaze to Keith.

'She was wearing a large size in men's Wellingtons,' Keith said, 'and she never got down off her tractor.'

'That's right, my dear. Until about the middle of February, as near as I can remember it, she was walking everywhere in her brogues. Very proud of her small feet, she is. But, ever since then, she's been going around in her Land Rover or on her tractor, and wearing a pair of her husband's old wellies.'

'So,' said the sergeant, 'she'd made up her mind to kill Joe Merson, rather than pay him off. When he saw what she was going to do, he tried to bring his gun up, but he only got as far as her feet before she blasted him. His gun went off, and she got it in the feet and ankles. She didn't dare to go to a doctor with gunshot wounds, just at that critical time, so she's been trying to nurse herself better.' He picked up the phone.

'Wait until I've finished,' Penny said reprovingly. 'I'm sure I don't know why you're in such a hurry.'

'There's more?'

'Just a bit. It must have been a terrible time for her. She looks ten years older, and no wonder. You could feel sorry for her, if it wasn't for what she's done. I *am* coming to the point, you don't have to be impatient. The vet was in here the other evening, chatting with a couple of farmers about drugs and antibiotics for cattle. He said that every farmer ought to keep a stock handy, just in case of injury to his beasts. He said Mrs Benton was a sensible woman, she'd been stocking up with things like penicillin spray although she doesn't have a single beast of her own these days.'

'Right,' said the sergeant. He grabbed up the phone and dialled a number.

203

Penny and Mr Enterkin clinked glasses. 'I'll have to put you to work in Newton Lauder,' Enterkin said. 'With you behind the bar in the hotel I'd have every case won before it came to court.'

'I'll go through and see if Mr Brown needs a hand,' she said, but she made it sound like a promise of eternal bliss.

'I gather,' Keith said, 'that you two intend to make a go of it. Despite what you've always said about the state of holy bedlock. I wish you happy.'

'Get those boots off her,' the sergeant was saying. 'If there's a doctor available, get him to examine her feet. I'll hang on.'

'Thank you,' Mr Enterkin said to Keith. 'I confidently expect it, but thank you for your good wishes anyway. Which reminds me.' He blinked at Keith. 'If you'll forgive my saying so, your marital boat seems to be rocking a bit. I trust that you haven't been getting up to any shenanigans again?'

Penny came back. 'They're telling blue stories through there,' she said. 'They didn't need me.'

'I wondered,' Keith said to Enterkin, 'whether somebody had been putting the poison in. About me, I mean, with Molly. She's been acting all week as if I'd been guilty of something.'

'Why would anybody do that?'

'I've been trying to think of a reason, and I can't. Except . . .'

'Yes?'

'There's the person who's been ripping-off Mr Grass with faked-up guns. If he didn't want me poking around the collection, he might have got somebody to phone Molly with a made-up tale, linking me with some bird through here. That could be it,' Keith said doubtfully.

Mr Enterkin pointed his finger, not very accurately, at

Keith. 'That is it! Somebody thought that if Molly was told that you were having an affair through here, she'd stop you coming back. They were, of course, living in a dream-world. Molly couldn't and wouldn't stop you doing anything, she'd just be hurt and say nothing.'

'I'll tell you something else,' Penny said. 'When Ralph and I started going together,' she managed a small blush, 'there was gossip went round of course. But for once they had it wrong. They thought it was you and me . . .'

'And yet another thing,' said Mr Enterkin. 'This morning, I had an odd phone call from Molly. She asked whether I had really telephoned you to come here, to the inn. Which suggests very strongly that somebody had got hold of that erroneous rumour and tried to use it to their own ends.'

'But that still doesn't make sense,' Keith said plaintively. 'It'd have to be somebody local. But the only reason would be to keep me away from the guns. And there isn't a gun-dealer around here.'

'There's Mrs Benton's brother,' Penny said. 'Waterhouse, his name is.'

TWENTY

The sergeant hung up the phone. 'That does it,' he said with grim satisfaction. 'She'd managed to get most of the pellets out, but the punctures were still weeping.'

'Just a moment,' Keith said. 'We're dealing with something else. Penny, did you say that Waterhouse is Mrs Benton's brother. Jack Waterhouse?'

'Yes.'

'But somebody told me she was a Cunningham.'

'Her mother was, my dear.'

Keith stared fixedly at the Glen Grant bottle for a few seconds. 'Now it all comes together,' he said. 'Put up another round while we work it out. Jack Waterhouse is a mad beggar, always coming round scrounging for guns that he can bodge up and sell at a profit. And he's a damn good engraver. In fact, if he'd made up his mind, he could have earned more as an engraver than he makes dealing dishonestly. But he's just the man to have pulled off those fakes and flogged them to Ray Grass. Great! This gets me off the hook with Molly.'

The sergeant was scribbling again. 'It also provides a better possible motive,' he said. 'Mrs Benton being broke was a motive, but there didn't seem to be any reason for her to decide to do the deed at that particular time. But if her brother had been faking up guns and selling them to Mr Grass, who had twigged it and demanded restitution which he couldn't give, that would be enough to push a loving sister, who'd probably absorbed most of the money anyway, into killing in defence of her brother.'

'One thing at a time,' Keith said. He looked at Enterkin. 'Suppose you ring Whinkirk House. Speak to Molly, if she's in. Announce your forthcoming nuptials. Then hand over to me and I'll find out if it really was Jack Waterhouse who passed on the word.'

Mr Enterkin thought it over, nodding solemnly. 'Good idea,' he said. He squinted at the telephone. 'Dial the number for me.'

Keith dialled the number. They heard the ringing tone. The three men put their heads together and Penny leaned over the bar; but the connection was a loud one and every word could have been heard across the room. Molly's voice answered. 'Hello?'

'Molly, my dear,' Mr Enterkin said. 'Tell me honestly, how are you?'

'Oh, I'm fine,' Molly said coldly. 'Just fine! You sound a little pickled, so I suppose Keith's with you.'

Keith closed his eyes. Mr Enterkin drew his lower lip out and down. 'We were hoping,' he said reprovingly, 'that you would come up to the inn and join us in a little party to celebrate my engagement to Mrs Laing.'

Even over the phone, they could hear Molly swallow. 'You?' she said at last.

'None other.'

'You're engaged?'

'I certainly am. And not before time, as you have been telling me for years.'

'To . . . to Mrs Laing. Is that the lady . . ?'

'The barmaid, my dear,' Mr Enterkin said. 'No need to avoid the expression. I do not find it opprobrious. Indeed, many of my happiest memories are associated with that calling – across the counter, I hasten to add. Suffice it to say that we clicked from the moment that Keith and I first entered the inn. She serves a beautiful drink, and who can ask more of a wife than that?'

He listened for a moment and then passed the phone to Keith. 'She wishes to speak to you, for some strange reason. Would you like us to withdraw? Not that we have the least intention of doing so.'

'Keith,' came Molly's voice. All the old warmth was back in it, and he felt his heart lift. 'Keith, is it really true? It's not just that he's drink taken?'

'He's getting rapidly stoned,' Keith said, 'but it's perfectly true. Listen, we've only just figured it out that somebody must have told you that it was me that was – er –'

'Keith, I'm so sorry.'

'Tell me later, in deeds, not words. This is urgent. Who was it put the poison in?'

'I promised I wouldn't tell you.'

'Was it Jack Waterhouse? It's important.'

'I couldn't see any reason why he should lie about it.'

'It was?'

'Yes,' said Molly, and she added, 'he's here now.'

'He's what?'

He walked in a few minutes ago and asked for you. I said you weren't in, and he said he'd wait.'

In the silence which followed, Keith had time to meet the eye of each one of his companions. He found no comfort in any of them. When he spoke again there seemed to be a hedgehog stuck in his throat. 'Is there anybody else in the house?' he asked.

'Not just at the moment. The servants went –'

'You've got to get out of there,' Keith broke in. 'It's vital. Get out of there without him seeing you and go and hide in the woods or something. I'll be right over.'

208

'I don't see how I can,' Molly said. 'He's waiting in the hall, and I'm upstairs in Miss Wyper's office. He'd be bound to see me come out of the corridor and cross the landing, which-ever way I went.'

'Is Miss Wyper's gun handy?'

'She took it out with her. There's only –'

Molly's voice was cut off in mid-sentence and a new voice cut in. 'Listen to me, Calder,' it said.

Listening to the nasal, slightly lisping tones, Keith could see the face and wondered now why he had not known Mrs Benton for Jack Waterhouse's sister. If nothing else, the arrogant, supercilious expression should have been familiar. 'Is that Jack Waterhouse?' he said slowly, while he thought. 'What are you –'

'I'm telling you only one thing,' Waterhouse said. 'If there's any one person in a position to meddle in my business, it's you. So I'm taking your wife away with me. You'll get her back next week if I'm satisfied that there's nothing coming over me and my sister. Otherwise, you'll get her back *all* next week, a piece at a time.'

Keith started to say, 'It's too late for that.' But the line went dead. He dialled the Whinkirk House number with frantic, fumbling fingers. There was a short but agonising delay and then the exchange signalled that the line was out of order.

The other three were looking at him, white-faced all. The sergeant began to get up. 'I'll come with you,' he said.

'No. You're injured. More use here. Phone your chiefs to send cars to Whinkirk House, fast. Waterhouse drives a rusty old Rover.'

The sergeant held out keys. 'My car.'

But Keith was already on his way to the door. 'Ten times further by road. And there's road works. Traffic lights. Quicker cross-country.'

Keith's last words were almost lost as the door swung to behind him. Brutus just managed to slip through the gap without losing his tail.

Keith was prepared to run all the way to Whinkirk House. He knew that it would take him all of ten minutes. That might be soon enough. Molly would fight like a tigress and it would take time to capture her, subdue her and get her into a car. But Molly should not be fighting. Molly was carrying his hope of immortality.

Outside the inn, Keith looked frantically around, for a bicycle, a tractor, anything that could shorten the time to Whinkirk House.

Miraculously, as if in answer to a prayer, the perfect, the only vehicle was near the door. A battered old Land Rover, and young Bert Yates just turning, with the keys in his hand, to lock the door.

Yates was never sure what hit him. By the time that he could sit up, winded and with the beginning of what was to become a specimen cauliflower ear, Keith was in the Land Rover, Brutus had dived across him and they were away.

Keith turned down past the general's house – God, the general, he'd go and see the old boy in hospital – and as he went he blessed the days spent walking the estate. For a Land Rover could cut across farm-land as no car ever could. Keith began to plot his route, while part of his mind remembered Molly, Molly at her most loving.

What had she meant, 'There's only –'?

Keith felt sweat on his forehead. He thought that it must be ninety proof.

Waterhouse might think that he had time in hand. And there were three separate drives from Whinkirk House. But Waterhouse might not know where Keith was phoning from. He might be impatient.

What had she . . . ?

St Cynthia's sacred twat! There was one weapon to hand in Miss Wyper's office – the triple-damned, four-barrelled, multiple-loaded Roman Candle. Surely she wouldn't? Yes she bloody well would! Keith slammed the Land Rover into four-wheel-drive and reduced the first gate to a memory. The general had called the Roman Candle a contraption, but that had been, if anything, flattering. It had been designed as the desperate last resort of a cornered man. In theory, the super-imposed loads should fire one at a time and starting from the barrel end, but Keith was a student of that part of history dealing with and affected by firearms. There were many examples. Rupert One-hand, Prince of Dresden . . . Keith could only thank whatever gods there might be that he had been interrupted before he could finish adding all its loads. He had been quite prepared to let the general take his chance, but Molly was different.

Keith's route that day took account only of impassable barriers such as ditches. Fences, gates and crops were as nothing beneath his wheels. It took a week to repair the fences, a month to restore sheep and cattle all to their proper owners, and a year before the marks of his passing were wholly gone.

Back at the inn, while Penny hovered anxiously and Sergeant Jim spoke urgently into the telephone, Mr Enterkin was thinking weighty thoughts, despite the haze induced by a substantial quantity of brandy on a stomach as empty as it was ever allowed to become. He was remembering his conversation with Keith in the car, after their meeting with Inspector Glynder. He remembered, too, Keith's proposal for financing a legacy to the inspector. And there came to him a new and superlative task for the inspector to perform at the service.

'They're on the way now?' the sergeant was saying. 'That's fine!'

Mr Enterkin put out his hand. 'If that is Inspector Glynder,' he said thickly, 'let me speak to him. I have some interesting news to impart.'

TWENTY-ONE

Keith had chosen his route with skill. His final approach to Whinkirk House was downhill on grass, and therefore with as much silence as Mr Yates' Land Rover could maintain, and finished up, screened by a thicket of flowering shrubs, a hundred yards from the gable of the servants' wing. He was out and running before the Land Rover had come to a halt.

At the edge of the gravel drive, he had to slow. He was reasonably sure that his arrival was so far undetected, and there was no point in throwing that advantage away. Walking gently, he rounded the corner of the house. To his infinite relief, Jack Waterhouse's car stood, unkempt as ever, by the front door. He thought of waiting in ambush behind it. But Waterhouse might have used one of the Whinkirk House cars, or might intend to do so. And Molly was in no condition to struggle.

The dining room window was slightly open. Keith pushed it up and rolled over the sill. Now he could hear a man's voice somewhere in the house. Between relief and the whisky his knees felt loose, and he steadied himself by the long table as he tiptoed towards the door. He was quite unaware that Brutus, infected by both his urgency and his caution, was padding softly along behind.

With the door opened just a crack Keith could be sure that the voice was that of Jack Waterhouse, and all the old antipathy came flooding back, increased a thousandfold by new knowledge. Gently, very gently so that neither sound nor visible movement nor sudden breath of air would alert the other man, he pulled the door open until, slow as a tortoise, he could ease his head through and take a look.

Waterhouse was standing at the head of the single flight of stairs that led up to the broad landing. He stood close to the wall, and was addressing his words towards the corner of the short corridor which led to Miss Wyper's office.

The stairs were thickly carpeted and, as far as Keith could remember, there were no creaking treads. He heaved a sigh for his gun, still standing behind Penny Laing's front door, and started up the stair on all fours.

'You may as well come out,' Waterhouse was saying. His voice was meant to sound calm and confident, but under the domineering tones Keith could hear a dangerous desperation. Keith saw that he had an automatic pistol in his hand, and he looked ready to use it. 'If anybody gets here soon,' Waterhouse went on, 'it will be your lord and master, and he'll get himself killed. Which might be an alternative way of solving my problems. Much better to persuade him to do it my way, by coming along quietly.'

'I won't,' said Molly's voice.

'Even to save your husband's life?'

'He's a better stalker than you are,' Molly said throatily.

'If that's old Grass's Roman Candle you've got there, I repaired it for him,' (*bloody liar,* Keith thought), 'and if it goes off at all, which I doubt, it's as likely to kill you as me. So I strongly advise you not to pull the trigger. I, on the other hand, am going to come round the corner in a few seconds, shooting.'

'If you kill me —'

'I can remove you all the more easily, and as long as your doting husband thinks you're alive he'll do what he's told.'

'It's too late,' Molly said. 'He's already told the solicitor, and there's somebody coming up from London.'

'If Calder buys the guns at face value, he's admitting that his first opinion was wrong. Think of it as a sort of ransom. Now, make up your mind.'

Keith had already made up his mind. As he arrived close behind Waterhouse, he was holding his breath in case the smell of whisky should betray his presence. He decided to hit the man hard behind the knees with his shoulder, as a preliminary to a good, old-fashioned thumping. In preparation, he retreated down one step.

His foot came down on Brutus' front paw.

The yelp of a stricken dog is intended by nature to be among the most startling sounds in the universe, and it ranks high among nature's more successful designs. The penetrating squeal jerked Waterhouse round as if he had been whipped like a top.

If Keith had jumped like a rabbit at Miss Wyper's shot that afternoon, his leap at Brutus' shriek was that of a gazelle, and as he came upright he began to throw up his hands to hold his balance on the stair.

The combined result of the movements of the two men was that as Waterhouse span round with the pistol outthrust, he placed it just above Keith's hands. Instinctively, Keith grabbed and held.

Immediately, they were locked in a joint-cracking tug-of-war which neither could afford to lose. Keith's prime preoccupation was to keep the pistol pointing away from himself. He croaked Molly's name, with some idea in mind that she might break the deadlock by batting Waterhouse over the head with the Roman Candle. Then, inevitably, the pistol fired. A blast of gas from the ejection port seared Keith's hand, and he felt the spent cartridge try to eject and stop against his fingers. He almost smiled. Nothing was going to fire that gun again for the moment. He dropped his hands violently, pulling Waterhouse across his hip.

In an attempt to save himself, Waterhouse let go of the pistol, grabbed for Keith's coat and missed. He landed, in a sitting position, half-way down the stairs and bumped the rest of the way to the bottom. Keith could hear his teeth snap together at every step.

Faintly but increasing, from outside came the double bray of an approaching police car. Waterhouse, winded as he was, staggered to his feet and made for the front door.

Keith dropped the pistol into his pocket and stepped round the corner.

Molly had heard Keith's voice call her name. She had heard the shot and the sound of a body descending the stairs. When a male form appeared suddenly in silhouette against the bright landing, she pulled the trigger.

Keith's life was undoubtedly saved by that extra tenth of a second lock-time that a flintlock takes to fire.

In the instant when she decided to pull the trigger, Molly also recognised her husband at the far end of the barrels. But a message once sent along the nervous system can not be called back. With a modern gun, Keith would have been dead. The Roman Candle was pointed between his eyes while the cock struck down at the frizzen, but Molly's hand was already jerking up. As the priming flashed in the pan, the gun was clearing the top of Keith's head, and the first shot passed him by to shatter a sporting print on the landing wall. As the gun spluttered its series of shots from the super-imposed loads, Molly's arm was still swinging up. The second ball went into the cornice. The third shattered a small chandelier in the landing ceiling, scattering crystal droplets down into the hall. The four remaining shots went through the corridor ceiling.

Keith groped his way forward through the thick pall of gunpowder smoke and took Molly into his arms. She leaned weakly against him.

'Keep it pointing at the ceiling.' Keith said. 'I've lost count. There may be another one up the spout.'

'All right.' Molly put her other arm round his neck and pulled his head down. She planted little, fluttery kisses over his face. 'Keith,' she said at last, 'I'm sorry.'

'What?' Keith's ears were still ringing. He had been at the noisy end of the gun.

'I said I was sorry.'

'For shooting at me?'

'No, that was your own fault for coming round the corner suddenly when you knew I was expecting somebody else. I'm sorry I believed what he said about you. Anyway, I'd seen him coming up the stairs with that Luger in his hand, so I wasn't waiting to recognise a face.'

The smoke was clearing. Keith pulled the pistol out of his pocket. 'Luger?' he said.

Molly looked down. 'No, it isn't, is it? Well, it looked like a Luger. It's a Finnish Lahti.' Keith opened his hand to let her see that the grips were black instead of brown. 'Swedish Model Forty,' she finished triumphantly. 'Can I put this one down now? My arm hurts.'

'Well done. What? Oh yes, it's safe now.'

Molly dropped the Roman Candle on the carpet and hugged Keith with both arms. 'I *am* sorry,' she said again. 'Truly I am. It'd have served me right if you'd found somebody else.'

Keith had spent a large part of the night in the bed of Bessie the maid, but this was not the time to remember such things. 'I'm a happily married man now,' he said. Which, at least, was true.

'And a respectable businessman,' Molly said. 'So you always say. And likely you'll make a good father. Most of the time. But, Keith, you go along fine for long enough, and then suddenly you'll go off the rails. The trouble is, you're irresponsible.'

A dribble of water started from one of the holes in the ceiling. It fell clear of them, and neither noticed it.

'Let's go home,' Molly said. 'Our own lives . . . house . . . bed. And the shop.'

Keith ran his fingers down her back, in the way that she always enjoyed. 'I'd like that,' he said. 'I've just about finished here. But I'd like to bide over for the memorial service. That's if you don't mind.'

'Why do you want to?' Molly asked.

Some flakes of plaster fluttered down behind Keith's back. 'I'll tell you,' he said. 'It's going to be a hoot. Apart from anything else, there's going to be what the papers call a startling revelation which was not in the will. You mind Alice Wyper and her rabbit-skins? She's not curing them half long enough. You know how nice and soft they feel before they're really cured and dry? She's stitching them up while they're still like that, and a neat fit she's making it, too.'

'They'll shrink when they get on the warmth of her,' Molly said.

'And she's using a fine nylon thread, and stitching the skins by their very edges. I think the stitches'll pull through and the whole thing'll come to bits.'

Molly thought this over and smiled. Alice Wyper's manner to Keith had been heavily flirtatious. 'All right,' she said, 'we'll stay over.'

A fresh trickle of water played suddenly over their heads. A chunk of ceiling fell nearby and water came pouring down. In seconds, the carpet was awash.

'Irresponsible I may be,' Keith said, 'but it wasn't me put a bullet through the water-tank.'

They clung together, helpless with laughter, while water and plaster rained down around them.